Life is Falling Sideways

by MICHAEL C. KEITH

ISBN: 0-9842489-0-0
ISBN-13: 9780984248902

Published by

PARLANCE

P.O Box 391114
Cambridge, MA 02139

For Curtis, Casey, Dwight, and Owen

ALSO BY MICHAEL C. KEITH

AUTHOR'S NOTE

THIS STORY TAKES PLACE IN 1954, A DECADE BEFORE THE CIVIL RIGHTS MOVEMENT WOULD HELP LIBERATE PEOPLE OF THEIR PRIMITIVE ATTITUDES AND PREJUDICES REGARDING MINORITIES, WOMEN, AND SEXUAL ORIENTATION.

FAMILY REMAINS MISSING

***Providence*—** Police continue to investigate the apparent disappearance of the Clayburgh family, who reside at 147 Belmont Street in the city's south end. Two weeks ago Calvin and Martina Clayburgh and their two children were reported missing by a neighbor. Reports that they may have been on their small boat in Narragansett Bay have been unsubstantiated and their boat has not been located. The investigation continues without any new leads at this time.

(*Providence Tribune,*
July 12, 1953)

Life is falling sideways
Jean Cocteau

Morning Rises

I sense there is something watching me from the darkest corner of my attic-room, following my every move. Something that should not be there. A toothy dead thing in a 3-D movie, ready to lunge at its helpless victim's neck. An hour, maybe more, passes before I give in to sleep again, and then almost instantly my alarm chimes, waking both me and my dog, Topper, who leaps from my side to the floor, farting loudly as he lands. When my dad hears him do this, he threatens to put a cork in it. I reckon that wouldn't be easy to do to a dog his size. It's time to get up and dress for school. The room is bright and the corner, where hours before something awful held me in its cold gaze, is empty, but I have a strong feeling that whatever was there is just invisible now in the sunlight spilling through the window.

As usual I have a stirring down below, what my goofy pal Henry calls a morning cukey, short for cucumber. Just before waking up, it feels like somebody is poking me between my legs with the handle of a broom. Another unpleasant dream, I figure, but when I reach down there, I realize what is happening. This has been going on for about a year, at least since I turned thirteen, and it's kind of uncomfortable, especially when I try to roll back over on my stomach for a few more winks before my mom calls me down for breakfast. When I do this I have to adjust my thing or, I swear to God, it feels like it's going to break in half. I wonder if that could actually happen and the thought makes me cringe.

"You got to do somethin' about it or it will stay that way all day," explains, Henry.

I know that is true because I haven't done anything about it in the morning yet and then I have to conceal the bump in my pants when I go down for breakfast. The idea of messing with myself down there as soon as I wake up seems like a weird way to start the day, but so is climbing out of bed with my diddle sticking out. When I stand on top of my bed to inspect the lump in the mirror, I can't help notice with some concern that my skinny frame magnifies the bulge. If my other muscles grew as fast as the one in my shorts, I'd soon look like Charles Atlas, I muse, flexing my puny arms. To avoid embarrassing stares when I enter the kitchen I place my schoolbooks over my fly area.

Henry takes this subject very seriously. For him, playing around with his cukey is his favorite activity, except for shooting baseball cards, and he's the champion at that. No one can flip a card like he can, but lately I've been winning more cards from kids than he has, and he says we're going to have a playoff to see who is the king of baseball card flipping in South Providence. I'm in no hurry to play against him, and if I do I'll hold back my most valuable cards and trade for more to replenish what he wins from me.

He beats almost everybody, even the bigger kids. Of course, everybody is bigger than Henry because he's a midget. In fact, he's a black midget. My father says he's seen a lot of colored folks and has even seen quite a few dwarfs in his lifetime, but he says Henry's the first colored dwarf he's ever come across. He jokes to Henry about it, but Henry isn't too happy about being told that he's such an oddity. I assure him that my father really likes him a whole lot, but that may be stretching the truth some, because my dad isn't too fond of colored folks in general.

Henry is one of the funniest kids I have ever known, and Corey and Bob think so, too, but sometimes they think he can be pretty disgusting, like when he marches around with his private out. When Bob expresses this view, Henry tells him he's just jealous because he has a tadpole in his boxers whereas he himself has a telephone pole.

Across the Divide

By the time I return to my room to put on my clothes
for school the stirring below has pretty much stopped,
but I know it won't stay that way for long since it has a
habit of rising every time I think of my friend Mary Kay
before she got sick or the pretty ladies in their under-
wear in some of my father's *True Detective* magazines.
I've discovered that when I look out of the window of
my attic bedroom to the empty house across the street,
the swelling goes down real fast.   It's where everyone
got sick and a little girl died. Sometimes before I leave
my room I take a quick glimpse at what my friends and
I call the Polio House and that does the trick.   Poof,
my thing goes back to normal but not for long.   I'd be
really embarrassed if anyone in my family, especially
my mom, saw me like that.

"David Ketchum, what is the matter with you?
For God's sake, behave yourself!" I figure she would
say, since that's her reaction most of the time when I
do something she considers really weird or stupid.   I
think seeing me with a morning cukey is something

she would definitely consider weird and stupid, if not revolting, too.

My bladder is nearly bursting since I haven't relieved myself yet, and I wonder if I can get away with peeing out the window like I do when it's dark outside. Our only bathroom is on the first floor and when I have to pee in the middle of the night I relieve myself by squirting out the window. Lately I have noticed a yellow stain forming on the side of the house, so I figure I have to stop doing this before it gets worse and somebody notices it. My father would be really mad, but it's just such a bother going down two flights of stairs in the dark to use the bathroom, especially in the winter when it's freezing in the house. I can see my breath in my attic room when it's really cold outside because it isn't insulated and the tiny radiator doesn't work very well, so I want to get back under the layer of covers as fast as I can.

Some mornings it seems tougher than others to get my motor going, and this is one of them. It's like my legs are slogging through freshly poured cement. After nights that I don't sleep too great everything feels like slow motion. Even the little sparrows that fly past my window act like they're bucking strong head winds. Before I drag myself out of the house my mother gives her usual warning about taking shortcuts.

"Take the main streets," she shouts from the kitchen, as I pull open the front door.

She has never gotten over the time I took a short cut to school and was grabbed by an old drunk, who went through my pockets and stole my lunch money. I haven't gotten over it either, so she really has nothing to worry about when it comes to my taking other routes to school. Besides, that was over two years ago, and I'm big enough now to take care of myself if that happens again. Any old bum would be picking on the wrong kid to rob if he tried it with me. I have learned how to defend myself pretty good with the help of my father, who knows some boxing moves, and my friend Corey, who learned some jujitsu when he lived in Okinawa with his mom, an airline stewardess.

When I'm out on the street I shoot a look at the Polio House hoping I will not see the dead little girl in the window like I did a couple of nights ago. When I got up to pee out the window, I swear to God she was there staring back at me. It made me leak all over the window sill and floor as I ran back to bed to get under the covers, and it took me forever to get back to sleep. When I woke up in the morning, she was gone. Maybe it was my imagination, but it seemed awfully real to me. I can still see her small face and its weird expression, like she was in pain, and it seemed like she was trying to tell me something. Maybe that she saw me peeing out the window.

The Polio House

The story about the Polio House goes something like this. Almost two years ago all the kids who lived there got polio and one, a little girl named Sara, died. This drove the parents crazy and they disappeared with their two remaining children, who were crippled by the disease. No one has heard or seen them since, and some say they went out into Narragansett Bay on the father's small fishing boat and died during a storm, but no bodies have ever been found. So the place is haunted. At least that is what I think, and most of my friends think so, too, except Henry, who thinks that idea is a bunch of baloney. He might be right, but I don't think so.

I'm going to move my bed, because where it is now I go to sleep looking at the abandoned house, and I swear to God it's looking back at me. The two-second floor windows are like eyes that stare right into my room. If I had a shade on my window I'd pull it down. My dad is supposed to put one up but he never seems to get around to it. Sometimes I hang my clothes over it but my mom says it looks bad and takes them down when I forget to do it. Then I end up with nothing to keep the Polio House from gawking in at me.

When I woke up in the middle of the night a couple weeks ago I saw lights on in one of the windows, and there was a shadow moving inside the room. It was small and I could tell it was her, the dead girl . . . Sara. When I reported this to my parents they said it was impossible not only because no one lived there any more but that the electricity was shut off. They told me I was just dreaming and letting my imagination go wild. While my mother shrugged it off, saying I should focus on all the other nice houses on the block, my father seemed agitated by my account and mumbled something about the house being the neighborhood curse.

"Don't let your imagination get the best of you, son," my dad said. "That train only goes one place—the nuthouse."

Actually, that wasn't the first time I witnessed something inside the house. Last winter when I couldn't contain my bladder anymore and had to get up to relieve myself out of the window I heard voices coming from it. Well, not exactly voices, more like moans and groans. As I was standing at the window trying to pee as fast as I could because the cold air was blowing in on me, the sound got louder. It made my pee stop mid-stream and for a minute I couldn't move even though I was freezing. Suddenly a light flickered from inside the house and the moaning stopped and everything was still. The wind wasn't even moving, and even though I had not finished peeing I sprang back under the covers and stayed there until I could not breathe and was all sweaty. Then I only poked my face out of the covers so I could get some air, and there was that old house staring in at me, and it looked angry and sad at the same time.

When I mentioned what happened to my parents they said the same thing about my dreaming and fantasizing, so I've decided that this is the last time I'm going to tell them about the weird stuff going on in the Polio House. Corey and Bob don't think I'm making things up or hallucinating as my sister claims.

Corey had his own creepy experience with the house when he used its back yard as a short cut to my house. He said he had just climbed over the fence when he heard someone call his name from inside the house. It wasn't a little girl's voice but a boy's. Probably belonged to the oldest son, we figured.

Anyway, as he ran across the yard to the driveway, he heard more voices coming from inside the house. There was screaming, too, said Corey, and a man's voice kept shouting, "Not to us! Jesus almighty, not to us!" When Corey got to the street, the voices stopped like they had suddenly been switched off, and the whole thing made chills run up his spine. Because of that he never stopped by my house but went directly back home to report the incident to his mom, who told him that his imagination was getting the better of him, too.

"You kids are just dreaming stuff up and letting it get the best of you. You're just making too much of that old house," she said, adding, "It was a sad thing what happened to that poor family and to make any more of it was just compounding the terrible sorrow that already existed."

What Corey's mom said to him was almost word for word what mine said to me. As usual my father just

cursed the place, calling it a damn eyesore and com-
plaining that it was dragging down the neighborhood,
which was already on the slide because so many different races were moving in.

"Maybe some decent white folks will buy the place
and clean it up," he said, adding that more than likely it
would just go empty because it was falling apart. "Looks
like it's going to topple over. It's a real blight, and with
all the nutty talk about it being infected by polio and
haunted by the Clayburgh family nobody will ever buy
it, except maybe some coloreds. Hey, then it really will
be filled with spooks," he joked, and I gave him a disapproving look thinking of my friend, Henry. "Well, that's
all we need living across the street from us. Maybe you'll
think differently if that happens, kiddo."

Sometimes when it's windy the Polio House seems to
wail like it's in pain and the harder the wind blows the
louder and more horrible it gets. Swear to god there
are times its gusty sobs keep me awake late at night.
Everything it does seems more intense in my room than
anywhere else in our house. It's like it has chosen to
bother me above everyone else, but I'm not going to let
it chase me out of my penthouse, as my father grandly
calls it. Even though Henry considers the whole thing
pretty stupid, he admits that there's no way he would
get up in the middle of the night to take a leak out the
window with that old house looking at his cukey.

Girl's Legs

From the time I moved to 146 Belmont Street I thought Mary Kay was the prettiest girl I had ever seen. The good witch in *The Wizard of Oz* could be her older sister, especially when she smiles. If they had a dimple contest, I swear to god Mary Kay would be the hands down winner, and if they had an award for the biggest blue eyes she would get it, too. She is still real cute even though her legs have been twisted up by polio, especially her left leg, which is bowed and brittle looking like a small branch that has fallen from a dead tree. Her face hasn't changed a bit, although it looks sad a lot since she got sick. Even when she isn't smiling, she is still prettier than anybody I know, even most movie stars, like Doris Day and Grace Kelly.

On my way to school I often stop by her house to say hello. She lives just down the street from my house at 123 Belmont Street, and her mom is friends with my mom. Because of her polio, Mary Kay has a tutor come to her house. Maybe next year she'll come back to school, says her mom, who looks like a grown up version of her daughter, because she has her big blue eyes and wavy blond hair, but not her dimples. What I like best about Mrs. Walton is her scent. It's like roses and something else that I can't really identify, but it's so sweet smelling that it makes me think of a bakery or a flower shop. She's also funny and always has something to say that makes me laugh. I can see why my mother likes her, but my father says she's a little kooky. Scatter-brained is how he describes her to my mother, but I think she is just kind of different, and I like that about her.

"Good morning, David. You're looking unusually handsome today," says Mrs. Walton.

Like my mother she calls me by my real first name but some kids call me Ketch, which is short for Ketchum, my last name. What I don't like is when some kids call me Ketchup.

"Mary Kay is in the kitchen having her breakfast. Come in," says Mrs. Walton, who is still in her bathrobe. It has a rip in the back, which seems strange because she makes a living sewing things with a large Singer machine in the living room. The tear reveals part of her underpants, and as she leads me through the house I can't help but stare at the hole. I can feel an unwelcome tremor in my midsection, so I look away as we enter the kitchen.

Mary Kay is listening to the "Salty Brine Show" on the radio and giggling at one of his jokes, "What kind of a ball doesn't bounce? A meatball." She smiles widely at me as I enter. Her legs are visible because her nightgown is riding up over her knees, and when she notices me looking at them she covers them quickly. They look like they don't belong to a normal size torso. I wonder if they will ever regain their regular shape again or if Mary Kay will look even weirder as she gets older, like she is standing on a set of badly warped stilts. When her braces are on, she can walk with the help of crutches, but she has to move very slowly or she could fall, so Mrs. Walton is never far from her in case that happens. When I visit she lets me take over this duty, but Mary Kay doesn't like to be monitored closely by me or her mother, claiming that she can do just fine on her own and that she doesn't want to be treated like a cripple, even though she is one.

"Hi Ketch," she says, pushing her half eaten bowl of corn flakes aside.

Her mother says she's going to get dressed and that we should have a nice visit. She then gives Mary Kay a kiss on the cheek and leaves the kitchen, the hole in her nightgown revealing even more of her underpants. Once again there is an awkward stirring in my lap.

"Don't get any more good looking, David. We don't want to lose you to Hollywood," jokes Mrs. Walton disappearing into the hall.

"I hate my tutor, Miss Cuttington," says Mary Kay gazing down at the half eaten bowl of cereal. "She treats me like I'm a third grader. Just because I have polio doesn't mean I'm stupid. I don't know why I can't go back to school now. I can walk okay with the crutches, and I feel fine."

"I got to leave to meet Corey and Bob," I say trying to avoid the subject of her not being able to do normal things. "We might play hooky today and hang out at the old factory . . . the asylum. Maybe your mom would let you out later."

"She'd have a bird if I left the house. The only time I can is when she's with me. Then we only go to the corner for exercise."

Changing the subject I report that our neighbor, Mr. Brennan, is still working on his boat, something he has been doing forever it seems, and that it should be finished soon.

"Maybe when it's done, we can all go for a trip out into the bay. Mr. Brennan says he's going to take us on its maiden voyage. You can come," I say and this cheers her up. "He says when the next hurricane comes, it's going to flood everything. The whole city of Providence will be under water and maybe even the whole state. His boat will have a motor so he can ride far inland away from the big waves that are going to hit. He figures he can get to the Connecticut line, and that will be far enough to survive. He'll have enough room for six people, so we can go with him."

"He's always saying crazy things that you can't believe," replies Mary Kay scrunching her brow skeptically. "But I would like to go for a boat ride when it's finished. Maybe I won't tell my mother if we go, because she'd never let me. So don't say anything, okay?"

With that I take my leave while Mary Kay remains seated at the kitchen table because she hasn't got her braces on yet.

"Why wouldn't the moron open the refrigerator door?" asks the voice on the radio. "He was embarrassed to see salad dressing."

Mary Kay likes that one and is chuckling loudly.

"Come by after school, if you can. Or after you play hooky, and we can work on the puzzle of the Grand Canyon."

Big puzzles are Mary Kay's favorite activity now, and every time she finishes one her mother has it lacquered and framed. The living room walls of her house are covered with them. The one I like best is of Paul Bunyan holding an ax in one hand and carrying a huge pine tree over his shoulder. He is one person no stupid polio germs could cripple, I think, as I inspect it on the way out of the house.

The Gang

Corey and Bob are waiting just outside the school-yard but well beyond view of any teachers or the principal, Mr. Walling. Bob looks like he has just fallen out of bed, but that is the way he looks most of the time. His brown hair shoots out in all directions and the buttons of his shirt are in the wrong holes making him look like he is standing on a slant. All in all he's pretty much a mess, as usual. On the other hand, Corey is always neatly dressed and groomed, although the sleeves of his shirts usually look like they are riding up his rapidly growing and hairy arms. He seems to have grown another inch every time I see him, and he towers over Bob and me even though we're all the same age give or take a few months. He really looks more like an adult than he does a kid, and he even has a beard. None of us has to shave yet, but he's definitely going to have to soon. We both admire Corey's mature appearance, because both Bob and I look a little younger than we actually are to start with, and that has its drawbacks. Corey's voice has changed, too, and it's deep like a grown man's. Ours still sound like kids, but my voice is starting to make the change to adulthood because lately it goes wacky in the middle of sentences like I'm trying to yodel, and that irks me because people laugh, especially my sister, who won't let it alone. I think Corey is the smartest of the three of us, too, though he doesn't like school much more than we do. He doesn't have to study a lot to get good grades, and skipping class doesn't seem to make a big difference for him. He always says weird but smart things, like "There's no sound on the moon because there's no air to carry it." I didn't even know it took air to make noises.

Bob is always excited about something when we meet, which is just the opposite of Corey, who never seems to get riled up about things. He's a lot more reserved than either Bob or me and listens far more than he talks. This is okay with us, because he's a great audience and always seems amused by our endless chatter and stories. Sometimes he just shakes his head and rolls his eyes at us when we're goofier than usual. We like to get a rise out of him, because he seems to try hard to keep a serious face.

Corey is the leader of our gang. We don't admit aloud that he's our leader, just like we don't admit we're not a real gang, at least not like the ones in the movies. He's the leader mainly because he is so much bigger than we are and doesn't act like a kid all that often. I get the feeling sometimes that Corey would rather be elsewhere—sometimes I think that his mind is already grown up and moved on. But we know he's our friend, even if he does treat us like we're his younger brothers. His size makes him sort of our bodyguard. When we're with Corey, I feel we have some protection against kids who like to bully people. It's not that Corey is a great fighter. He's not. I mean I've never seen him in a fight. In fact, he avoids bullies as much as we do, but his appearance and big person's voice is a enough, so they don't seek him out like they do us. School is full of kids that just want to make life miserable.

Before the school bell sounds signaling everybody to go to their assigned homerooms, we head off to the place we call the asylum to meet up with Henry, who steers clear of the school grounds entirely because the principal is after him, or so he claims. Apparently he whacked a kid who was making fun of him, and his teacher sent him to the principal's office. He's had to stay after school all week and wash the blackboards as punishment, so now he vows never to return.

"Didn't do nothin but defend myself is all. Nobody's gonna' call me a tar baby and get away with it. Don't matter if they're white or God, I'm gonna' kick their ass. Get them like the Mau Mau."

The only thing Henry says he likes about going to school are the air raid drills because he gets to look up girls dresses when the class is told to duck and cover under their desks.

To reach the room we call Headquarters, we have to shimmy up a drainpipe to a boarded window, which we've managed to pry open enough to climb through. We each clutch a flashlight so we can find our way to what we call the shock room. It's where we figure crazy people were given jolts of electricity because it has all kinds of wires and a platform in the center on which stands a panel with meters and knobs that look like something out of Flash Gordon. It doesn't work, but we like to take turns fooling around with it and pretending we're about to launch the whole building to Mars.

"My mother had electroshock treatments, but it only made her worse," revealed Bob, whose mom is crazier than a drunken bed bug. She lives at home with him and his older brother, Mark, who is a big creep. He's always yelling at Bob and his mother, and sometimes he smacks his brother. Bob just seems to take the crummy situation in stride, like his is a perfectly normal family, but I think deep down he knows it's not. He never complains, even when I witness first hand his brother's cruelty or his mother's weird behavior.

"They're okay. You get used to it. Mark just acts up sometimes. He gets that way when he drinks," explained Bob, but I think his brother is a lousy jerk who just enjoys beating up on him.

His mother is another thing though. She doesn't know what she's doing and is completely out of her gourd. She gives me the willies because you never know what she's going to do. Once I dropped by to pick up Bob and she started screaming and flew at me with her fists swinging. That time both Mark and Bob had to carry her back to her chair and calm her down while I escaped to the doorway of their apartment. It really scared me. I had never seen a woman's face look so mean or so wild, like some kind of batty witch. Now when I come by to get Bob I always keep a safe distance from her in case she explodes again. She never takes her eyes off me and mumbles curse words like I'm her worst enemy.

"She won't hurt you. Don't worry. Strangers upset her, but she only acts like she's going to do something.

She never really does," explained Bob while stroking her forehead to soothe her out of her spell.

According to Bob, she got crazy after her husband died in a bus crash that involved a bridge abutment and an icy road. She used to be like other mothers, he says, even nicer than most.

"She was so nice you would think she was the best mom in the world, and she really was."

To me, it seemed that Bob's life changed for the worst after that happened, because he has shown me photographs of the house he lived in when he was very small. It was huge and had beautiful flowers all around it. The place he lives in now is pretty much a dump. It's over a radio repair shop in a neighborhood my father says has completely gone to the dogs.

"It's full of spooks and spics and no place you want to be after sunset," observed my father. "Our neighborhood is going to turn brown."

My father is racist and says "those people" a lot when referring to basically anyone who doesn't look like him.

"But, Dad," I say. "Henry is one of *those* people."

"Your friend Henry is an exception," my mom says. "Right, Don?"

"I don't think I'd go that far," replies my dad. "The whole damn area is becoming a slum, which means this house won't be worth a fig if we ever try to sell it."

The inside of Bob's apartment is just as dreary as the outside. All the furniture looks real old and the upholstery is torn on the couch and chair in the front room, which overlooks the blinking neon sign for the store below. It is cluttered with old newspapers and magazines and there usually are dirty dishes scattered about the place. It kind of smells, too, like a combination of vomit and beer.

Bob shares a bedroom with his brother, who has taken to covering the walls with pictures of girls in scanty bathing suits and hot rods. Mark has a bed but Bob sleeps on a ratty sofa under a window that looks out onto an alley filled with old garbage cans. Bob says that when he is in bed at night he can hear rats chomping at the contents of the dented and overturned cans.

"Some of them are gigantic, like cats," he says. They make weird noises, too."

When I suggest that they may in fact be alley cats, Bob directs my eyes to the carcass of a large rodent rotting among the scattered debris. There is no mistaking it for a cat, that's for sure. Bob and his brother use the oversized rats for target practice with the Daisy BB gun strategically propped against the wall next to the window, and the dead rat is the result of their sharpshooting.

"We each shot it," boasts Bob. "It took about a dozen BBs to kill it. The first shot stunned it, and it just froze in place, so it was easy to hit but not to kill. Even after all the BBs we put into it, it still flopped around for a while. Mark heaved a beer bottle at it and that finally did the job."

As much as I love animals, the idea of killing rats does not bother me all that much, but I would not care to watch them being pulverized by BBs and bottles. I don't think anything should suffer, not even something pretty disgusting like a giant garbage eating rat.

When we reach the shock room, we cast the beams of our flashlights in all directions to make sure it is safe to enter it, not that it's ever unsafe, but part of our game is to move through the abandoned building like it is enemy territory and we're on patrol. We inch along the hallways, listening and watching for what will leap out at us as from one of the mysterious rooms at any moment and do us deadly harm.

The Asylum

We know we are trespassing and that makes us nervous, except for Henry. "You guys are chickenshits," he says. "Whose gonna' care if we're in here? Nothin' worth stealin'. Just a big ole empty building that nobody cares about, so at least we're giving it a use."

When I remind him that there are "no trespassing" signs posted all over the building, he replies that they only put those signs up to keep kids like us from having some fun.

"You just afraid 'cause you know they're ghosts in here. Zombies with lightin' bolts comin' out their heads, 'cause they was zapped, and it killed them. Maybe that little dead girl from the Polio House is here, too, Ketch, and she gonna' get your skanky ass once and for all."

The place does give us the heebie-geebies, and we know that deep down Henry is just as scared as we are, but he likes to act like nothing ever bothers him.

At one point in the dark corridor that leads to the shock room, Henry gives out a loud bloodcurdling wail, and Bob nearly jumps onto Corey's shoulders. My heart pounds so hard I think it's going to break my ribs, and we all shout at Henry to stop acting like a jerk. Meanwhile, he is laughing so hard he can hardly catch his breath, yet he manages to make a monster face that is really creepy because his head is so much bigger than his stubby body.

The asylum was a state run home for the insane until a few years ago when it was shut down because a new facility was built on the other side of the city. Since then it has stood empty in an area of South Providence that has a lot of other old stone and brick factory buildings that look kind of fallen down. A couple years ago its windows were boarded up because they had been broken by kids chucking stones through them. Bums also used the place to camp in until the cops cleared them out.

Bob's mother was a patient at the asylum and after it shut down, she was sent home. That left Mark and Bob to care for her and themselves. Of all of us, Bob likes being in the asylum the least, and he only agrees to enter when he knows there is no way to convince us from doing otherwise. To compound his unhappiness about being in the abandoned building, we have chosen the shock room as our headquarters. It took us a long time to get him to join us because he believed his mother was given shock treatment in there. According to Bob, his mother was much crazier when she left the asylum than when she entered it, and he figures it was probably the electrical charges that ruined her for good.

"I'm not kidding, when she got home her eyes glowed in the dark like tiny light bulbs. The juice was still in her noggin' and has never left. If you put your head next to hers you can still hear the electricity humming."

When we reach the door to our headquarters, Bob hesitates as usual and we have to convince him to enter along with us.

"What're you afraid of now? Ain't nobody in there. Sure ain't your mama's sane self. That part was fried by all that juice they stuck her with," says Henry leading the way into the room.

With Bob huddled between Corey and me, we enter our designated command center and immediately start fiddling with the broken control panel.

"Too bad nothing works. It would be fun to see what this machine would do to my aunt's nasty cat," says Corey shooting the beam of his flashlight at one of the meters and tapping it with his forefinger. "It might make her more friendly. It couldn't make her more nuts. Every time I go to my Aunt Lola's house, that cat arches her back and hisses at me. I gave her the boot once when my aunt wasn't looking. Then things just got worse with her. My aunt says she's fine with every one else. Just wacky around me."

"This electroshock would make her even crazier," comments Bob as Henry ignites a bunch of matches that momentarily light up the entire apparatus and casts our shadows eerily against the room's high walls.

When the matches burn down close to Henry's fingers, he tosses them on the floor and ignites another batch. Corey stamps the matches out with his foot while shouting at Henry not to do that because the dry wood floors will catch fire.

"That'd be somethin'," says Henry, with excitement in his voice. "This ole place would make the best fire you ever saw."

With that he chucks another bunch of burning matches to the floor, and Corey punches him in the arm while warning him not to do it again or he will suffer even greater consequences.

"You keep your big ole mitts to yourself you fat Commie, or I'll tell my mama and she'll beat on your fat white butt."

Henry's mother is gargantuan, kind of like a walking mountain, and his threat is not to be taken lightly. I found this out the hard way when I first met Henry and we got into a fight in the schoolyard because he said he heard my sister showed an older boy her titties, adding that he thought she had a classy chassis, too. That did it! I got him on the ground to make him take it back, and his mother showed up out of nowhere, lifted me off her son like I was a feather, and threatened to break my neck if I ever touched him again. Not too long after that Henry and I became friends, and now his mom likes me and I like her, although I know enough not to make her mad.

"Can you smell the fudge?" asks Bob, and all of us except Henry say we can, although I'm not really sure if it's chocolate we're sniffing or the burnt match sticks smoldering on the wood floor.

"I guess that means we're all crazy then, "adds Bob, referring to the story about how asylum patients reported the scent of fudge even though there was none being baked anywhere in the building.

The really weird thing about it is that the asylum was a chocolate factory before it was converted to a crazy house. Reportedly, it was closed down because some people were poisoned by the fudge they made there. My mother says she's not sure about all the details but that she heard something like that actually did happen back in the early 1930s. All she recalls is that two people supposedly died when an angry employee put arsenic in the fudge to get back at the owner for something he did to him. Ironically, a few years later that same person ended up a patient in what then had become the loony bin, and he claimed the odor of chocolate was suffocating him, although none of the staff people could detect anything unusual about the air in the place. Apparently soon after many of the other patients also complained of the same breathing problems and that led to the place being shut down and a new facility being built somewhere else.

"I don't smell nothin'," says Henry haughtily, "so that must mean I'm the only sane man here, but any fool would tell you that."

"Maybe you're the only one who *is* crazy," says Bob, sniffing hard at the air. "I mean, if you're the only one who can't smell the fudge, it could be that you're the real nut."

"Smell this," says Henry, who sticks out his butt and makes the sound of a loud fart. "Whoa, maybe you're right. I do smell the fudge now," he adds, making another fart noise.

The Gargoyles

We stick it out in the asylum until school is out to avoid being seen by the truant officer. We have played hooky before by hanging out on the roof of the Biltmore Hotel, which we have appointed as our official downtown headquarters. It was there that we conceived the idea of our club–The Gargoyles, named after those weird figures sticking off the top of buildings. Corey came up with it because he likes reading about old buildings and castles that have Gargoyles hanging off them. Membership requires that we walk the rooftop ledges of skyscrapers, the taller the better. The idea behind this ritual is to demonstrate to one another our worthiness to be a part of such an exclusive order. It makes us feel unique and special, something we don't feel around the kids at school who think we're geeky and ignore us.

Corey is the most daring of us. He's had less fear than me on any day. I'm not afraid of heights, I'm just cautious in general. It's my father's fault. On the other hand, Henry has refused to take part in our ledge walking calling us a bunch of white fools. He hangs out with us when we search for other buildings to test ourselves on, but he refuses to go within several feet of a roof's edge. He prefers the dark rooms and corridors of the asylum.

"The crazy people's ghosts may getcha' in here, but at least you don't smash all over the ground with your brains and guts bein' splattered everywhere," he says with his right eyebrow arched in disapproval.

We have tried to get on the roof of the asylum but the opening to it has been so securely shut that we have given up trying to break through it. There are large planks of plywood nailed across the door leading to the roof, and we figure they were put there when the asylum was in business to keep the inmates from escaping or jumping to their deaths.

There is one place we avoid in the asylum because it spooks us out. It's the dining hall and what makes the place so scary are the shadows that flicker through the cracks in the boarded up windows. They make the large room seem occupied by awful spirits, the walking dead as Bob suggests. Corey says the moving shadows are probably caused by pigeons flying around outside, but he suggests we should steer clear of the place because something doesn't seem quite right about it to him either. His idea is enthusiastically embraced when we hear a strange noise coming from what we conclude is the kitchen at the far end of the dining hall.

"They be the devil in there," remarks Henry, as we close the door tightly behind us and scamper down the hall to the shock room where we feel more at ease and less intimidated by this strange dark land that gives us refuge from the boredom of school.

"I ain't coming here no more," says Bob, when we reach our headquarters room. "This place is bad, and something's going to happen to us. I'd rather find someplace else to hang out."

"Look!" shouts Henry, pointing to something behind Bob, who screams and clings to Corey. "It's a wall," he says laughing, "A big ole ugly wall."

"I think I just loaded my pants," says Bob, and we all practically topple to the floor in hysterics.

Later when we emerge from the dark recesses of the asylum, the brightness nearly blinds us. We have had enough of our dreary and creepy hideaway to appreciate the rewards of the sun-drenched world that zombies and vampires avoid.

Confessions

Sleeping late is the best part about the weekends, but lately my eyes open at sunrise and I can't go back to sleep. Fact is, I keep feeling like I'm being watched. It's as if someone is in my room, and I know it's because of the Polio House and the dead little girl called Sara. Maybe it's all in my head, but it really seems like there is something or someone staring at me, and it wakes me up with a bad feeling.

Although I try to avoid looking at the Polio House, my eyes just automatically wander to it. It's like I can't help myself. I'm drawn to it like a nail is to a magnet, and it upsets me that I don't seem to be able to do anything about it. Although I hang some of my clothes over the window, I can still detect its presence. It seems to defy any attempt I make to ward it off or block it out. Then there's the weird noises and stuff late when I'm trying to sleep.

My sister, Linda, thinks I'm nuts when I report these things to her. It was a mistake to tell her because as usual she treats me like her silly little brother and that really goads me because she is not that much older than me, only a year-and-a-half, but it might as well be ten the way she acts. Like a big shot she offers to sleep in my room and lend me hers, but I 'm not about to sleep in there with all the pink pillows and goofy stuffed animals. I'd feel like a pansy if I did, because it's such a girl's room, and I wouldn't be comfortable. The only attraction about her room is its closeness to the bathroom, but even that is not enough to get me to spend the night there. Besides, I figure once she gets my room she will want to keep it so she can smoke her cigarettes without risking being caught by our parents whose room is next to hers.

Her teasing me about my ghostly concerns causes me to finally reveal what Henry said he saw her do with a boy. It's not something I planned to ever tell her, but now I'm so mad that I spill the beans.

"I know you showed your knobs to a guy," I say and this makes her eyes practically pop out of her head.

"What! My . . . what?" she exclaims, her face turning beet red and her eyes narrowing to angry slits. "Who told you that? That's disgusting. You have a dirty mind, and I'm telling mom."

"Go ahead," I say, confessing that it was Henry who reported her indecent act.

"What does that little coon know?" she practically screams at me, and I tell her she is disgusting for using that word for a friend of mine. "You should stay away from him. He's nothing but a liar, and his mother is a tramp. I hear there are always all these men coming in and out of her house."

"She has two brothers, and they visit her a lot and do chores for her because her husband is dead or something. That's all the men you see at her house. She's really nice and always reads the bible, too," I say, defending Henry's mother.

"Well, that runt is bad news, and I don't want him in this house because he always looks at me weird."

"Maybe he wants to see your knockers, Beanie Lulu," I say taunting her with the goofy name of her imaginary friend when she was little, and she pushes me out of her bedroom and slams the door in my face. "Beanie Lulu, Beanie Lulu!" I shout at the closed door.

After this clash we don't talk for several days, and I begin to feel bad for the things I said to her. This is another thing I will add to my list of sins to take to confession. It must be a pretty big sin to say such terrible things to your sister, even though it may be the truth. So maybe it's not a sin after all or just a little venial sin that doesn't require a long act of contrition, maybe a couple Hail Mary's.

This is something that occupies my mind the rest of the day, and by the time I enter Father Carter's confessional booth I'm anxious to be forgiven for my meanness but afraid of the harsh lecture it might inspire from the priest.

When I fess up to the things I said to my sister, he asks for more details.

"Did you see her do this to the boy?" he inquires, and I say no.

He then asks if I have done anything sinful with another person, and again I say no.

"Have you touched yourself in a sinful way, my son?" continues Father Carter, and I hesitate before I answer in the affirmative.

"What have you done, my son?"

I confess that I jerked off, and then he asks something that really surprises me.

"How did it feel?" he asks, and I reluctantly admit that it felt pretty good.

There is a long awkward pause as if the priest is thinking about what to ask me next and when he does speak he tells me to do five Hail Mary's and six Our Fathers, which is a lot less than I expected because he has told me to say many more prayers in the past for things that were not as bad as saying nasty stuff to a sister and wanking. After he doles out my act of contrition he tells me to come by the rectory sometime soon to further discuss my sexual transgressions, as he calls them. It is something I am not about to do, and I hope he won't come by my house or call my parents when I don't respond to his request.

Going Up

Corey and Bob claim they have been asked similar questions by Father Carter, and they also have been told to visit him in the rectory to discuss their sex sins. Like me they have no intention of meeting with him and plan to avoid his confessionals in the future, which won't be easy since he is the only priest at St. John's.

"He's creepy," observes Bob. "There's no way I'm going there by myself. Maybe we should all go together."

"He wouldn't go for that. He wants to get us alone," says Corey.

"What do you think he'd do?" I ask, and Corey and Bob shrug their shoulders.

"My brother says he used to ask him about sex, too, during confessions when he used to go. He went to the rectory when Father Carter told him to but won't tell me what happened when he did. He just says I'll find out if I go," reports Bob.

"Do you think he's a homo?" I ask, and Corey and Bob shake their head yes.

"Maybe we should make up some sexy stories to tell him for the fun of it," I suggest, and Corey and Bob think it's a great idea.

"Yeah, lets tell him we had sex with a bunch of girls. We got blow jobs and all that kind of stuff," says Bob.

"What if he tells our parents?" I ask, and Corey says that there's no way that Father Carter is going to say anything to them.

We agree that the next time we go to confession we'll make up some whoppers to tell him, and we'll see how he reacts. We devise separate accounts of how we did dirty things with girls and to ourselves to really get him going. Bob wants to tell him how he had sex with a dozen different girls even though we know, like us, that he has never had sex with anyone but himself. I say I plan to tell him that I jerked off ten times in one day. Always a little more secretive about things, Corey says he doesn't know what he'll confess to but that he'll let us know when he comes up with something good.

On Saturday nights following confession we usually meet to head to a small liquor store on Broad Street in the hope of buying some wine. We have done this before, but tonight Corey is going to try to buy the booze himself. We have convinced him that he looks old enough, and we really think he does. Even though he is barely fifteen, he already has the outline of a beard, and because of his size he looks much older than we do. Besides his voice sounds like a grownup's and that is a real advantage.

In the past, we have had bums buy us wine by giving them enough money, usually seventy-five cents, to buy a bottle for themselves. When we approach the liquor store, Corey gets cold feet, but we assure him he will pull it off without a hitch. The worst that could happen is that the clerk will say no, we tell him, and he agrees to give it a shot. We stand in the shadows outside the store and watch as he selects three bottles of cheap wine and takes them to the cashier.

The clerk takes the money from Corey without even looking at him and in seconds he rejoins us with our prizes. We are thrilled with his success and congratulate him, but Corey responds to our enthusiastic praise in a very matter-of-fact manner like it was no big deal, but it actually is. We each have our own bottle of Thunderbird burgundy and in the alley next to the liquor store we uncap them and take our first swig, which is always the hardest for me because I hate the taste of booze. Bob is the only one of us who seems to really like the taste of the wine, and he takes a prolonged gulp. When we have done this in the past, he's usually the one who gets much drunker than we do, even though we also have finished the contents of our bottles by the end of the night. We're baffled why the same amount of alcohol affects him so differently.

Our plan is to head to the roof of the Biltmore and do a little Gargoyle ledge walking. It is a rule of our club that we do this at least once a week. If we fail to do so, then we're supposed to lose our membership in the club, although there are weeks we don't fulfill this requirement because we can't gain access to another roof we consider worthy of our efforts or we just forget to do it.

The alley door to the stairs leading to the Biltmore roof is almost always unlocked for some reason, and it is there that we are able to meet the key requirement of our club's bylaws. However, on this night we get so loaded before our ledge-walking that we decide to just sit on the edge of the roof and gaze at the lights of the city and the stars, which always seem much brighter when you're on top of tall buildings above the street lights.

For a couple of hours we tell stories and talk about what we're going to be when we grow up. Corey is not sure what he wants to be, maybe a sailor, and I say I'm going to be a veterinarian, because I love animals, especially dogs, more than anything.

"You got to work on snakes, too, you know, if you're a vet," says Corey, and I say there's no way I'll do that given that I hate snakes. "I think you got to treat all kinds of animals, snakes included, to be a real animal doctor" he responds, and I say there are snake doctors just for that, not really knowing if there is.

"I'll treat animals with fur but not scales," I quip, and Corey observes that there are some pretty disgusting things with fur, like skunks, for instance.

Bob says he thinks he wants to own a liquor store or maybe become a psychiatrist. He can hardly pronounce his words, and it cracks us up when he gets hopelessly stuck on the word psychiatrist so that it keeps coming out "psychia*thrist.*"

Clearly enjoying the fact that he is the object of our amusement he staggers to his feet and makes a feeble attempt to climb up on the roof's ledge to do a little walking. Before he can mount the ledge, we grab him and drag him to the safer recesses of the roof all the while telling him he is going to kill himself.

"Who cares if I fall," he slurs as his mood suddenly turns somber. "Nobody will miss me."

We keep a firm grip on Bob until he seems about to konk out. Then we put his limp arms over our shoulders and start our long descent to the street and our trip home. Along the way, we stop at the Haven Brother's Diner for a hot dog, so that by the time we reach our respective houses, we are pretty sober. Bob stays drunk much longer than we do, and because he's still soused and can hardly stand on his own, we escort him all the way to his apartment to make sure he gets there. At his door he mutters something that sounds vaguely like "dwadillypod" and then leans against it with a loud thud produced by his head hitting it.

Brotherly Hate

When Bob enters the apartment, his brother comes charging to the door and pulls him inside with a ferocious tug. He reminds me of a fierce guard dog, with his lip drawn above his long gray teeth and his eyes glaring with anger. He slams the door after giving us a look that sends chills up my spine. We can hear him screaming curse words at Bob and accusing him of being a lush, which strikes us as ironic considering we never see him without a beer in his hand.

"You frigging little jerk. Who the hell do you think you are getting sloshed at fourteen years old?"

Bob shouts for his brother to shut up and let him go, and this is accompanied by a loud crash and then more yelling by his brother.

"You better stay locked in the bathroom 'cause when you come out I'm gonna' really kick your puny little ass," screams Mark, and then silence descends as we move back through the dimly lit hall leading to the entrance of the building.

"Somebody ought to set him straight about picking on his brother," I say, and Corey agrees, adding that the only way to keep him from beating up Bob is to lock Mark in a room with his crazy mother and throw away the key.

"They could kill each other, then Bob wouldn't have to deal with them," he says clenching his fists.

We stand outside the building for a few minutes eyeing the window to Bob's apartment, but thankfully all remains quiet. Whatever affect the wine has had on us has disappeared by the time we head home. When I enter my house, Linda is in the living room trying to follow the fuzzy images on the TV and my parents have apparently gone to bed. She looks at me with a smug smile.

"I saw you and your dopey friends outside of Broad Street Liquor. Corey had a bag with bottles in it, and you guys went into the alley for a drink."

This sets me off, and I ask her why she's not out showing off her big knobs, which aren't all that big anyway, I surmise.

"I'm telling mom and dad," she responds, her expression hardening.

"Yeah, and I swear to God I'll tell them about what you do with guys," I warn her.

"I swear to God! I swear to God!" she spits back mockingly. "That's all you ever say," and I have to admit she's right.

After our clash, she says nothing more to me staring straight ahead at the snowy images on the TV screen.

"Beanie Lulu," I say giving her a raspberry as I head to my room.

"Spaz!" she retaliates.

On the way up the stairs leading to it, I believe I hear dead Sara's voice uttering my name and chills run up and down my back. As soon as I enter my room I flip on the light switch and quickly scan it fearing that she is waiting for me with a butcher's knife. To my great relief the room is empty, and as usual I try not to look out the window in case she is floating inches away from it.

It takes me longer than the usual long time to get to sleep. Most of the time after drinking wine I go out really fast. Tonight, as much as I try, I can't keep from peeking out from beneath my covers to the openings in my clothes I again drape over the window. Every so often there appears to be something moving outside. I reason that it is probably just a tree limb turning in the breeze, but I have a deep and gnawing suspicion that it's more than that. Despite the fact that the booze is already working on my bladder, I am not about to open the window for a pee tonight. I'd rather explode in bed than be sucked out of the window by an angry ghost.

Wash Your Hands

The summer may be over but the risk of getting polio still exists, although it is not as great a threat when the days turn colder. As much as my family likes warm weather, we are all relieved when the chillier days of autumn arrive. My mother, whose main objective in life seems to be guarding us against the terrible disease, still insists that we take tons of precautions to keep the paralyzing virus away from our doorsteps. Among other things, this means we must avoid crowds and public places, especially toilets. Topping the list of things to do to keep from getting polio is washing your hands, and my mother is like a drill sergeant when it comes to this. She has us disinfecting our hands with Borax soap ten times a day until our hands are red and raw.

Henry says his mom is nuts about this, too, and he thinks it's all a scheme to keep kids from enjoying themselves. He has his own theory about getting polio.

"The only way you can get polio is by eating turds. You know, you got to actually eat crap to get it," he says, and when I ask him if he means that everyone ever stricken with polio were crap eaters, he says that somewhere along the line they must have swallowed turd germs. "There's poop on everything, my mama says. So that's why we gotta soap up our hands so much. You're eating turds even when you pick you teeth. That's why you gotta keep you paws out your mouth. Your cukey is different though. It's so nasty ain't none of them polio germs gonna' survive when you wrap your hand around it."

For the last three summers we haven't been allowed to go swimming at Lincoln Woods, where we used to spend three days in a small nearby cottage every July. It was always the high point of the summer for us, but now we just hang around the neighborhood in the sweltering weather until school starts again. Even a trip to Rocky Point, our favorite amusement park, is discouraged by our parents for fear of being exposed to large public crowds.

When Mary Kay came down with polio the summer before last after what happened to the Clayburghs, we were lucky to leave the house and play with our friends for weeks after it, because my mother was so terrified that we'd be next. That's when she really became crazy about our keeping clean and avoiding places where polio germs were known to breed, like at the water fountains in the park where we often went wading. We were told never to take a drink from the bubblers either, and what really hurt the most is that we couldn't set up our lemonade stand on Elmwood Avenue like we did most summers to make money for the movies and stuff, because everyone was afraid to drink home made stuff sold by kids.

Parents would panic whenever their children exhibited polio-like symptoms. Now parents panic when a kid comes from school with any symptom that could possibly mean polio. At the first sign of a fever, stomachache, or muscle pain the doctor would be called and you would be confined to your bed with your concerned parents buzzing around you like flies. Most of the time it was nothing, because kids were always getting aches and pains, but everybody feared the worst, and some poor kids, like Mary Kay and Sara and her brothers, got it, which makes me wonder why some people have bad luck and others have good luck.

Mary Kay almost died during the first several days of her polio, and then she spent months in an iron lung because she couldn't breathe on her own. Her whole body was limp as a washrag, and she couldn't lift her legs or arms. One day she was fine and the next day she was being rushed to the hospital because she was burning up and couldn't stand on her own. It really scared everyone and even Henry was at a loss for words, and that's incredible.

It was around that time that my dad began drinking more beer than ever before, and my mom wasn't very happy about it. Dad has started drinking more beer than usual—a lot more beer. And mom doesn't like it one bit.

"Balls McCarthy, Jessy, you're going to become an alcoholic if you keep drinking like that," she would complain using her favorite swears, and he nearly always answered her with these words: "Three beers does not an alcoholic make."

"Well, that's 21 bottles of beer a week, or nearly a hundred a month counting the extra days, and that puts enough alcohol in your blood stream to qualify you as one" she would counter, to which he would take a long gulp of beer and let out a huge burp.

That would make her say Balls McCarthy again, causing my dad to back off because he knew my mom was really irritated when she repeated her curses. It had become a familiar routine around our house. All in all, my parents got along with each other fine, but it seemed that every polio season, every summer, there would be increased tension between them, which me and my sister attributed to their fierce concern about our becoming sick and crippled or maybe even dying.

Polio was the big bad bogeyman that haunted everyone, even parents, who were much less likely to be its prey. The empty Clayburgh house across the street just seemed to make things worse, because it served as a constant reminder, or symbol, of just how terrible the effects of polio could be on a family. It seemed to bother my father more than any of us, even though he was not the apparent target of its ghosts like me. It was its falling apart appearance that really riled him more than any possible ghosts.

A Better Father

Other things kind of haunted my father. He had
a lousy childhood and his early adulthood was greatly
effected by the Depression. His parents were dirt
poor and lived in a small cold water flat in Dorchester,
Massachusetts. At fourteen he had to leave school
when his father had a heart attack and couldn't
deliver ice anymore because his strength had left
him. His mother worked when she could as a cleaning lady but her earnings amounted to pennies and
the family was nearly destitute, so my father had to
chip in to keep them from ending up on the street.

His jobs were always menial, not up to his abilities
and brains, which were really humongus, as my mom
would say, but he did what he had to do and didn't complain. When he was eighteen he met my mother and
they were soon married. At the time her parents, the
McKennas–or the "harps" as my father jokingly calls
them even though he's part Irish himself–had recently
moved to Pawtucket, Rhode Island, and they moved
in with them hoping to find better opportunities away

from a city that had never treated them very well. Not a long time later they were able to get a place of their own a few blocks away because they both had jobs. My father worked in the maintenance department at Brown University and my mother worked as a maid at the Narragansett Hotel on Weybosset Street in downtown Providence.

Linda was born first and then I came along about a year and a half later. By the time we were pretty grown up the apartment had become way too small, so with money my parents managed to scrape together over the years by working overtime and weekends, they put a small down payment on the house we have now. Owning the house is their biggest achievement and their most valuable possession, besides my sister and me, says my mom. Having their own place was a dream come true, and it took some of the disappointment out of the fact that their jobs had no status or glamour. The main thing was they could pay the mortgage and provide their son and daughter with the basic necessities of life, as they called them. That seemed enough for them. If it was not everything they had ever hoped for out of life, it seemed to come pretty close.

My dad reminds us all the time how much better we have it than he did when he was our age. He says there were times when all his family lived on were the stale handouts he could get from a neighborhood bakery in Dorchester, and for those he had to sweep up the place after closing time.

"You kids will graduate from school like your mother. I didn't get there. Finished eighth grade and that was that. Had to leave to help put bread on the table. Of course, I'm in college now and have been for over fifteen years," he'd joke referring to the length of his employment at the university where he had risen to the rank of foreman of the grounds crew. "Maybe they should give me a diploma, because I sure have spent enough time on that campus."

My mother was going to attend nursing school but decided to put it off when she got married to my father. After we were born, any thought she had of becoming a nurse went out the window. It was all she could do to squeeze in occasional cleaning work because of the demands of child rearing and my father's long hours at his job. She spent most of her time with Linda and me and despite her disappointment about not furthering herself professionally, she always said we were her greatest success and that as long as we were happy, she was fulfilled as much as anyone could be, including any nurse.

"You have to find your happiness where it exists, and mine exists with my family," she would often say with just a hint of resignation and regret in her voice.

Lately my dad's happiness level has been on the slide because of his worries about the neighborhood going bad. He doesn't like the fact that colored people and foreigners, mostly Puerto Ricans, are moving in. He thinks this is a major danger to property values and personal safety. Up until two years ago the only colored people living near our house were Henry and his mom, who had just moved here from down south, and that didn't please my father a whole lot, but he kind of came to accept them, especially when I became good friends with Henry. Now there is another colored family on the next block, and two blocks away there are two Spanish families, and he is not about to accept them.

"When these people move in decent white folks who can afford to move out do it, and your house is worth a lot less," complains my father, and when I remind him that he works with some colored guys, he says that's different. "It's one thing working with them, but living with them I can do without. Everything I have is invested in this house, so I don't want to see it go down the drain, but I guess there's not a damn thing I can do about it. When they start to move in, it spreads like the plague and before you know it the whole area is a worthless slum."

"Henry's mom keeps her house beautiful," I observe, to which my dad adds, "She's one in a million. Go any place where there's a lot of coloreds, and you'll see how things have gone to hell."

His gloom over the decline of our neighborhood is the biggest reason he is drinking more beer, I figure. He has been pretty upset since his favorite team, the Boston Braves, moved to Milwaukee, but the way the neighborhood is going is what he mostly gripes about.

Hitting Home

It keeps happening, and I think I might really be going nuts, because in the middle of the night I hear more noises coming from the Polio House. Not voices exactly, more like mumbling and soft crying. It's probably just my imagination, like everyone says, but it seems very real to me. A few hours after I fall asleep it starts, and I wake up with a start. It lasts for several minutes and during that time I am paralyzed by fear, not that I would get out of bed anyway if I could move. Eventually, I go back to sleep and when I wake up in the morning I am not sure whether I dreamed the whole thing or if it actually happened. My sense is that it was no dream.

While trying my best to hold down the upward motion of my morning cukey, I throw on my pants and shirt and head to the kitchen where I encounter my mom drinking her coffee and looking very pale. In the last couple of days she has not been herself, moving around like cement blocks are dangling from her waist. She is slumped over her cup at the table and doesn't notice me when I enter. The kitchen radio is playing a Perry Como tune, which is all it ever seems to play.

"Are you okay?" I ask, and she shakes herself out of her fog and reports that she has a headache and didn't sleep very well but otherwise is fine.

"Did noises keep you up?" I inquire, and she asks what noises.

Rather than get into the whole thing about the Polio House, I just change the subject, and fortunately she doesn't pursue it any further.

As usual I stop by Mary Kay's on the way to school. This morning she is dressed and waiting for me on her front porch. Her skirt nearly covers all signs of her leg braces as she stands with the aid of wooden crutches. For a brief moment as I approach she looks like she did before she got polio and I'm surprised, because I haven't seen her out of her wheelchair since she got home from the hospital. A broad smile covers her pretty face and her head is held high. This is an important moment for her, I figure, and I tell her she looks great.

She thanks me for stopping by and plants a kiss on my cheek and in the process of moving toward me my hand accidentally grazes her breast, but instead of pulling it away instantly I keep it against her until she moves away. Her face reddens but instead of being upset, which is what I expect, she looks at me sweetly and we gaze hard into each other's eyes. My thing is going crazy.

Once the spell is broken we stand and talk for a few minutes, until it becomes apparent that she needs to return to her wheelchair, which is strategically waiting a few feet away. Her courageous little display has taken a lot out of her, but even though she is exhausted, the smile never leaves her face.

"I'll be walking soon," she tells me as I help her back into the wheelchair, "Then I'll be able to do things and maybe go back to school. I'm going to surprise my dad when he gets home. I'll walk right up to him."

I tell her that it will make him real happy and ask when he is due back from overseas. He's a Merchant Marine and is sometimes gone for a half a year or longer.

"I'm not sure. Not for a while, I guess, but that will give me time to get better to surprise him," she answers, a big grin on her soft peachy face.

I promise to hang out with her this Saturday when her mom takes her to the park.

"We can go on the swings," she says, her eyes sparkling with enthusiasm.

"Sure, maybe the seesaw, too, huh? I add, and she looks like she is going to burst with joy.

At school I meet with Henry, Corey and Bob during recess and we play baseball cards until Henry has cleaned us out. Feeling sorry for us he insists we take back two cards apiece, but he chooses which cards these are, and they are not exactly among the best ones we lost.

After school he gives us a chance to reclaim our losses but within minutes, he cleans us out again.

"You boys playin' with a major leaguer and you're still in little league," he taunts us while wrapping a rubber band around his day's substantial winnings.

We make plans to meet at the asylum after we check in at home and then we go our own ways. I'm surprised to see my dad standing on the porch when I reach home, and I immediately assume that something is the matter.

"Your mother is in the hospital," he informs me, and when he tells me why I feel a blast of cold air flow from the direction of the Polio House and into my heart.

Henry's World

After two days my mom is allowed to return home. She has non-paralytic polio, I'm told, so apparently all she needs is some bed rest and plenty of liquids.

"If you got to get polio, it's the one to get," remarks my father looking like he has just removed a ton of bricks from his shoulders.

The doctor says she'll make a full recovery and should be back to her normal self in no time, maybe even in a couple of weeks. My father is so pleased with the outcome that he has pledged to never drink a beer again, and this makes my mom very happy.

However, she is not happy that my sister and I have been exposed to her polio germs and insists that during her convalescence we stay with friends. Even though her doctor says that is not necessary, she cannot be persuaded to let us remain in the house until she is completely out of the woods, as she says. My sister doesn't mind and quickly lines up a place to stay with one of her girlfriends.

On the other hand, I run into trouble when I check about staying with Corey, because his mother is away on her stewardess job a lot, and she does not allow Corey to have anybody in the house when she's not there, even though he gets to stay at home alone.

Bunking with Bob is out of the question because of his crazy mom and rotten brother, so it comes down to Henry, and my father is very reluctant about my staying with colored people.

My mom intervenes claiming that Mrs. Gilroy is an excellent person and it will be fine for me to stay there, if she will have me. I quickly check with Henry and his mother is delighted to take me in, but my father still remains cool to the idea even though he gives in to it.

Later in the day I take a small suitcase with a couple changes of clothes with me to Henry's house, and his mom greets me like I am a long lost and beloved relative. Even though I have been on good terms with her for quite a while, her enthusiastic reception is in such contrast to my first unpleasant encounter with her when I was fighting with Henry in the schoolyard that I have serious doubts about whether the person before me is one and the same. After all, this is the woman who threatened to break my neck if I ever laid a hand on her son again, and now she acts with such sweetness and affection toward me I am surprised and a little suspicious, too. For a moment I think that maybe these black people just want to get me into their house to do me in, but then I feel bad about even having that dumb thought.

"It's good to have you with us, David" she says, wrapping her thick black arm around my shoulder and guiding me into her home.

Henry's house looks a lot like my own, except for a lot more furniture. It is nearly impossible to move around the living room without bumping into something, yet it is very cozy and welcoming. Adding to this pleasant feeling is the smell of something delicious coming from the kitchen.

"Mama's making her fried chicken for supper and it's better than anything you ever ate," says Henry with pride and growing excitement.

We go to Henry's room where he immediately takes out his stash of dirty magazines from the dark recesses of his cluttered closet. About an hour later, his mom calls us to supper and I have one of the tastiest meals ever. Mrs. Gilroy keeps loading our plates, which we continue to clean until we are close to exploding. In her apron she reminds me of the smiling colored woman on the maple syrup bottles. Aunt something. When I mention this to Henry, he arches his eyebrow and asks if I mean "Ain't you mama?" Then the name comes to me, and I correct him.

"Aunt Jemima," I say, and he says, "Right, ain't *you* mama because it's *my* mama."

I don't really get his joke but I chuckle along with him anyway to be polite, which is what I need to be as a guest in his house. Later we cram into the living room and watch a TV show about two cowboys forced to ride on one horse because the Indians killed the other while Mrs. Gilroy folds a stack of freshly washed clothes. Television viewing is not a pleasant experience at my house, because the old one we have is mostly on the blink. My father has promised to replace it, but we don't know when. Linda doesn't care as much as I do because she likes to listen to her record player, but there are very few things I'd rather own than a television with a clear picture like the Gilroy's have.

I'm sleeping in with Henry who keeps me awake with stories he claims he has made up about soldiers and gorgeous women. They are very entertaining but soon I fall asleep despite his narrative about a guy with hands that become flame-throwers when he is battling the Reds.

That night I dream that my mom is in an iron lung that won't fit through the door of our house. There is mounting panic about getting her inside because something awful is approaching–a monstrous tidal wave is casting a shadow over everything. When my mom starts screaming, "Look out! It's coming! It's coming!" I wake up and listen to my heart pounding until sleep overtakes me again.

In the morning Henry yanks off under the covers while I pretend to be asleep. As he lets out an orgiastic grunt his mom opens the door and tells us to get our clothes on and come eat breakfast so we're not late for school.

"Shhiitt!" exhales Henry when his mom leaves. "That was a close one. Mamas ain't supposed to see that."

Dying Little

Henry had a brother who also was a dwarf. He died at four years old not long after Henry was born. He had climbed inside of a disposed icebox, closed the door, and suffocated. At the time his family was living in Alabama. His dad disappeared, and Henry believes he abandoned them because he just couldn't deal with the situation. He hasn't been heard from since, and Henry is still pretty sad about it.

"Mama told me papa always said life is fallin' sideways, so you gotta' be ready to catch onto somethin.' Guess he caught onto a train out of town, but who cares anyway?" reports Henry continuing after a reflective pause. "I was supposed to die little like my brother, but then I had an operation and now I'm going to live till I'm twenty-eight," he reports.

"How do you know you'll die at twenty-eight?" I ask, and he says because it's five years more than his doctors predict.

"They say I'm goin' to the lord in my early twenties, but I ain't going until my late twenties so I can get married at least three times. Besides, who wants to live until they're thirty anyways? You can't do this when you be that old," says Henry, who points to the ever-present bulge in his crotch. "When you're that old the cukey don't work no more, so you may as well be dead. Don't know why they call them stiffs when they can't get one."

I tell Henry that he'll probably live to be a hundred, and he says he thinks so, too. There may be another operation he can have when he gets a little older and is full grown, around four feet tall, he says.

"Gonna be the only hundred year old with a morning cukey," he jokes, and I wonder if his head will continue to grow to where it's twice the size as the rest of his body and how he'll be able to stand and move around if it does.

On the way to school we pass my house and find my father standing in the doorway as if he is expecting us.

"Hi guys," he says and reports that my mom is doing much better and I can come home pretty soon. "Hey Henry, you playing pocket pool?" he says to Henry, who has both his mitts jammed deep in his pockets.

"No sir. My hands are cold, Mr. Ketchum" he responds.

My dad says for us to drop by after school and he'll give us money for Yoohoos.

"Don't get lost on the way to school," he adds, and we get his meaning.

Actually, we have made plans to play hooky and hang out in the asylum with Corey and Bob, but now I have second thoughts. Missing school again so soon after our last absence may get us into trouble even though we have excuses forged by Corey, who can match anyone's handwriting, so I suggest that we wait to play hooky until next week instead.

"You're the biggest chicken, Ketch. Just because your ole man says something, now you're afraid," says Henry, and I respond that I just don't want to cause trouble while my mom is sick with polio.

Corey and Bob agree that we should hold off playing hooky for a while since we just did it. Henry is not happy with our decision and stomps off in the direction of the asylum alone. Before the bell rings for the start of school, he returns saying that it's no fun cutting school in a place with electro-shocked ghosts without his friends, even if we are a bunch of pale panty waists.

Besides Henry says he's concocted a trick to play on Miss Pinkerton, a teacher who he has had several run-ins with. His scheme is news to me even though I have been staying with him. He's removed the whipped cream from the contents of a package of Hostess cupcakes and replaced it with toothpaste. His skill at rewrapping the package amazes us, but we advise him against pulling the prank because we are certain he'll be caught. That's not about to happen, replies Henry, because he's going to leave them on her desk when she's not at it. He has carefully copied the handwriting of a girl in his class that he hates and has taped "For my favorite teacher" on the package.

Our handwriting expert, Corey, admits this his forgery is convincing. We ask Henry what kind of toothpaste he used and he tells us it is what his mama uses on her teeth so they don't fall out.

"That's not toothpaste," observes Corey. "It's glue. It holds her false teeth in place."

"She could get real sick if she eats that stuff," remarks Bob.

"So then she'll croak," replies Henry. "That way she won't be fussing with this man no more."

A few days later we hear that Miss Pinkerton had to have her stomach pumped out because of a horrible trick perpetrated by someone at the school. We wait for the boom to drop on Henry, but it never does. In fact, we learn that her ex-boyfriend, who it turns out is the school custodian, has become the prime suspect.

"Ain't that the funniest thing you ever did hear?" asks Henry, as I pack my things for my return home. Six days staying at Henry's house has been fun, especially because his mom is such a great cook and his TV has a clear picture, but I'm more than ready to take up residence back in my own room, ghost or no ghost.

On my way out of the front door Henry says to come back anytime that I want a penis butter sandwich. His mom catches his comment and orders him to spend an hour in his room without the use of his record player or radio.

"See the trouble you be makin' for me, Ketchup" says Henry with a pinched expression on his large face as the door closes between us.

I wonder what the world would have been like had his older brother lived and conclude that it probably would have been twice as much fun with two crazy colored dwarfs as friends.

Back Home

My sister is already home when I arrive, and she actually seems slightly pleased to see me, although we don't say much to each other. After not seeing her for a while, it strikes me that she is not as homely as I thought. In fact, I kind of understand why guys might want to see her without her clothes on, although the idea makes me want to barf. She has spent the week at her friend Brenda's house, which is one of the nicest in the neighborhood because her father is an accountant with a big office downtown.

They have a 21-inch Admiral television with an outdoor antenna, she reports. Our old Muntz never works very well because one of its rabbit ears is broken. I tell her that Henry has a good TV, too, even though the screen is small like ours. We decide then and there to push the issue of a better television set and will waste no time in doing so. At supper we will double-team our father on the subject and will be told that paying our mother's doctor bills is a higher priority. Besides the television picture is coming in better since he wrapped more aluminum foil around the twisted antenna, he says. We check it out and to our chagrin cannot detect any genuine improvement.

Our first glimpse of our mother is a little disturbing because she has lost weight and is not all that steady on her feet, but she reassures us that she feels fine and is ready to resume her life.

"Thank god it wasn't the bad kind of polio or I wouldn't be standing here. I'd be in a wheelchair like poor little Mary Kay," she says, and I inform her that Mary Kay can now walk with braces.

"Your mom is going to have to take it easy for a while, so you kids are going to have to chip in around the house a little more than usual," says my dad, who is sipping on a soda pop.

He is sticking to his promise to quit drinking beer and this has him behaving a little edgier than usual, I think. In fact, he is zipping around the kitchen like a deflating balloon prompting my mom to tell him to sit down because all his motion is making her dizzy.

"Balls McCarthy, honey, take a breather, will you? You're making my head spin."

"Sorry. Just excited you're home," responds my dad turning to me.

"So how was it staying with coloreds?" he asks, and I report that Henry's mom is a fantastic cook and that their house is very nice.

"Geez, I don't know about eating off the plates of colored people. Wouldn't be crazy about sleeping between their sheets either," he says, wrinkling his nose like he's just gotten a whiff of something smelly.

"They're just like us, dad," I protest, and he says he's not convinced of that.

"They come from the jungles, and it never really leaves them. They got some weird ways of living that ain't like decent white people."

"They pray more than we do," I offer, recalling how Henry's mom insisted on saying grace before each meal and was constantly reminding us to say our prayers before we went to bed.

"That's because they were converted from being godless heathens by white missionaries," replies my father spearing a chunk of the meatloaf he has made.

Frustrated by his comments I renew the issue about our broken television saying that Henry has one that has a great picture unlike our snowy set.

"That doesn't mean nothing," replies my father. "She probably got it from one of her boyfriends, and he probably stole it."

Later in the evening, when I reenter my attic room after being away for so long, the cold air it contains penetrates me to the bone, and it occurs to me that I forgot to tell my dad that colored people also have rooms with heat. Topper is already curled up on my bed, and even the smell of his farts isn't as bed as the icy currents that drives me under the blankets with all my clothes still on. I imagine my room is like a crypt in the deep of winter, a place of frozen corpses and ghosts of dead little girls.

Bless Me, Father

Henry thinks the Gargoyles is a stupid idea, so he doesn't hang out with us anymore on Saturday nights. He says he is not against the booze part but feels we should have our heads examined for walking on the ledges of tall buildings.

"Why you boys want to die? Ain't no way I'm gonna' go flying off the Biltmore and hit the ground like a fat watermelon. Shhiiiit, that's more stupid than what white folks normally do. What you fools tryin' to prove anyway? That you're dumber than you look?"

I guess we are trying to prove something by our high wire stunts. Maybe it just makes us feel special and not like the wimps that the kids at school think we are. It's really the juniors and seniors who want nothing to do with us, although our fellow freshmen act less than eager to become our friends as well.

"They're better things to do with my time," says Henry jerking his cupped hand back and forth.

Since he's not Catholic, he doesn't attend confession with Corey, Bob, and me either, but when we reveal our plan to play a trick on creepy Father Carter, he wants in on the scheme. First he has to learn what to say once inside the confessional booth, and this becomes a big challenge, because he can't seem to remember all the words.

"Damn, I'll just be tellin' him my sins, so to heck with all the 'bless me father cause I been sinnin' stuff. Just gonna' tell him I got a cukey job from a nun and he's not gonna' care if I get all the dumb words right when he hears that."

We are not sure that his participation in our plot is such a good idea fearing that it may cause Father Carter to blow a gasket and get us all into deep trouble.

"Don't need to play no dumb trick on some ole fairy priest anyway," says Henry, finally giving in to our pleas that he not accompany us to confession.

"Satan's gonna get your silly asses, but ain't grabbin' mine. No sir, ain't grabbin' mine," he says, shaking his head dramatically and acting like he's relieved to be excluded from the conspiracy.

We each have come up with what we're going to confess to the priest. Corey is worried about his deep voice, but he says whispering makes him sound younger, so that's what he's going to do. Besides, everybody whispers in confession so people outside the booth don't hear their sins. He's going to tell him that he has a venereal disease called the clap from having sex with several prostitutes, and Bob is going to claim that he does gross things to a doll. We kid him that he's not supposed to be confessing the truth. I plan to tell Father Carter that I have made three girls pregnant.

On the steps of the church our courage begins to falter and it takes a few minutes for us to reclaim our guts to go through with our hoax. Corey is the first to enter the confessional and when he emerges a few minutes later he has a huge grin on his face. Bob is reluctant to go next, so I do. After I ask the priest to bless me because I have sinned, I let rip with my account of impregnating several girls, all high school freshman like me.

"Were they virgins?" the priest asks and then tells me to explain to him exactly what I did with them.

When I simply respond that I had sex with each girl, he wants to know more. He wants details.

"Were you both naked, my son?"

"Yes," I say, and he asks what we did next. This requires me to rely even more on my imagination, since the closest I ever got to doing anything sexy with a girl was touching Mary Kay's breast.

"I laid on top of her and put it in her thing," I contrive with appropriate remorse."

"And what *thing* was that?" asks the inquiring priest, whose voice grows more intimate.

"Her . . . ah, you know, father," I answer.

"No I don't, my son."

"Her virginia, father."

"You mean her vagina?"

"Yes, Father. That's it," I answer.

"Did you ejaculate in her, my son?"

"Yes," I answer when it dawns on me that he is asking if I came in her. "That's why she got pregnant."

"Did you do the same thing with the other girls?" he asks, and I detect a shuffling sound coming from his side of the screen. "That is, did you do it the same way . . . I mean, in the same position?"

When I answer in the affirmative to conceal the fact that I'm not entirely sure what he's asking me, his inquiry ends with a long breathy silence. This is followed by his telling me to do five Hail Mary's and six Our Fathers. Again, it strikes me as a light Act of Contrition considering all I have confessed to, and I'm disappointed by the apparent ineffectiveness of my phony account.

Bob has lost his daring and leaves the church before I have completed performing my penance. He is sitting on St. John's steps with Corey when I exit the candle-scented house of God and Father Carter.

"I just couldn't lie to a priest," he says as I approach, adding that doing so must be one of the worst mortal sins a person can commit.

Corey and I tell him that it's more like a venial sin when a priest is a fruitcake like Father Carter, but he doesn't buy our reasoning, and I begin to feel that what we did may have some bad repercussions when we reach the gates of heaven and our sins are reviewed to determine if we are worthy of entering the Pearly Gates.

Out of Thin Air

There's a new clerk manning the cash register at the liquor store and Corey does not want to risk getting caught trying to buy wine, so we decide to get a bum to do it for us. We have done this a couple of times before. It requires we chip in about a quarter each so that the derelict can buy himself a bottle, too. Within a matter of minutes we spot a likely candidate and pitch our deal to him. Things go without a hitch and clutching our bottles of Thunderbird we are on our way to the roof of the Biltmore. It is Gargoyle Club night.

Bob is more quiet than usual, and he has a small bruise under his left eye and a scratch on his cheek.

"Got in a fight with my brother," he tells us, and we know it was more a beating than a fight.

As usual by the time we reach the Biltmore we are feeling the effects of the cheap wine, and Bob's mood has improved considerably.

"Dwaddillypod," he mumbles repeatedly, a ridiculous grin transforming his somber expression, and we ask him what the goofy term means. "Dwaddilypod," he says, his grin widening. "It means . . . dwaddilly-goddamn-pod! Don't you get it, you thilly cootie-heads?"

We don't but we choose not to press the issue further and climb our way to the roof. Bob lags behind us murmuring his mysterious word and giggling intermittently. He is pretty shloshed.

Our first view of the lighted Providence skyline always thrills us and for several minutes we stand silently and gaze in appreciation at the magical night scene before us.

"There's a dwaddillypod," shouts Bob, pointing in the direction of the Roger William's statue perched high up on College Hill.

Although the statue is hard to define on the horizon because of the darkness, eventually we discern its outline, but by the time we do, Bob is identifying dozens of other objects as dwaddillypods, while leaning precariously over the edge of the roof.

"Watch out, Bob. Back up or you're going to fall," shouts Corey, and when we move in Bob's direction he climbs onto the roof's ledge.

"Get off!" I yell, and he tells us to keep away.

When we move closer, he threatens to jump.

"I will. I mean it! Keep away! Dwadilly-fucking-pod!!"

He is weaving as he stands on the three-foot ledge of the roof, and it now strikes me that he could be drunk or mad enough to jump, or just plain fall.

"Please come down, Bob," pleads Corey, and Bob starts bellowing his cryptic term over and over.

"Dwaddillypod to you! Dwadillypod to them! Dwaddillypod to every shittypod out there!" he says sweeping his hand across the city's landscape.

While he does this we remain fixed in place fearing that he will act on his threat to jump. At the same time it seems more likely he will become airborne accidentally because of his drunken weaving or from an unexpected blast of wind.

"I don't want to live anyway. They hate me, and I hate them," slurs Bob.

"Who hates you?" I ask.

"Everyone," he says. No one says anything for a minute. Then Bob says, "My mother and brother."

"We like you," says Corey, and I agree adding that we're the three Musketeers, the Gargoyles, and without him we don't have a club.

"Yeah, you're our best friend, Bob, and you can come stay with me and my mother," offers Corey, and I make a similar gesture.

"You can stay with me in the attic, Bob. It would be great because that little dead girl's ghost is giving me the major creeps, and I sure would like you there with me when she comes calling again."

"The little dead girl . . .? Oh, yeah . . . from the Polio House," says Bob, finally grasping my meaning. Really?" he asks, and we tell him that he can stay with either one of us for as long as he wants, even though we both know our parents wouldn't allow it.

"Oh, shitty-dilly-dwaddilly-fucking-poddy, why should I die for them? They wouldn't even care," says Bob, all but falling back onto the roof.

"Dwaddilly-shitty-pod!" we all shout when he has returned from his near encounter with death, and then we take a long robust pee into the air swirling around the Biltmore.

Girls Like to Dance

Bob says he's going to deal with things at home and will not need to stay with us, at least not now, and we are relieved that we won't have to deliver on our promise to take him in.

"The next time my brother tries to push me around I'm going to take my bat to his head," says Bob, the effects of his wine consumption still mostly at work by the time we get to his house.

"Yeah, give him a knuckle sandwich," says Corey waving his clenched fist.

We confirm our plans to meet up for a movie the next day and part company.

"Dwaddilly-pukey-pod. I think I got to barf," responds Bob and clutching at his stomach disappears into his gloomy building.

Even though it's kind of late, on my way home I drop by Mary Kay's to say hello. Her mother directs me to their living room where I find Mary Kay practicing walking with her braces and crutches.

"You're doing great," I say as I observe her wobbly strides.

"I can do nearly ten steps," she says with considerable pride. "Each day I try to add two more steps. Next month I'll be able to walk around the block, and in two months, I won't need my wheelchair at all."

"That's fantastic. Maybe you can go on the maiden voyage of Mr. Brennan's new boat. He's going to launch it soon," I say encouragingly.

"My mother would have a heart attack if I did that. She'd never let me, but maybe I could come watch it put in the water."

Mary Kay has reached her physical limit and collapses into the wheelchair parked next to the sofa. She has to fiddle with her braces so she can bend her knees.

"I hate these things. Some day I won't need them," she says, struggling to get her impaired limbs onto the footrest of her wheelchair.

"I bet by next year you'll be perfect again," I reassure her, and I think she is almost perfect even with the shiny metal rods enclosing her crooked legs.

If she didn't get polio I would still think we should get married when we grow up, and I think we might anyway if she gets her legs back to normal. Of course, this sentiment is something I've never really expressed to her, but we both know we've always been practically girlfriend and boyfriend, and I can't imagine it being otherwise. I think about copping another feel of her breast but suppress the urge feeling that I might be pushing things so soon after the first time. Besides, what I'd really like to do is feel-up her butt, but that will have to wait until the right moment, and this is not it, especially since she's back in her wheelchair. I wonder if doing that to a cripple makes me some kind of creep, but I think it doesn't because I really like Mary Kay, and I know she likes me.

"Do you still see Sara Clayburgh at night?" she asks, and I confess that while I always sense her presence that it has been a while since she's appeared to me full fledged.

"Maybe that's it then. She's never going to bother you again. It could have been just weird dreams anyway. Sometimes my dreams are so real, I'm sure they are. I keep dreaming I'm dancing to Swan Lake. You ever see that?" she asks, and I admit that I have not. "It's so beautiful, and I'm one of the swans. When I wake up, I'm sure my legs are fine and I can dance."

"You'll be dancing just like one of those a big birds real soon," I tell her, and she chuckles.

"Not a big bird but like a *swan*. They're the most graceful creatures in the whole wide world."

I repeat the word swan for her amusement and satisfaction while wondering why animals don't get polio like humans. If they did, I would dedicate my future career as a veterinarian to finding a cure for a disease that would prevent beautiful birds from flying and wild horses from running.

Double Vision

It's Sunday and we are going to take in a double
feature of 3D flicks at the Capital Theater on Westmin-
ster Street. Bob announces he is a dime short of the
thirty-five cent admission, so Corey and I come up with a
nickel each for his ticket. The double bill includes a
new Vincent Price horror film called "The House of
Wax" and "Bwana Devil" about lions killing and eating people in Africa. All during the first movie, Henry
makes creepy noises and keeps saying that dead Sara is
under my seat and about to grab my gonads. When I've
finally had enough and tell him to shut up, two bigger
kids in the row in front of us tell him to do the same.
That shuts Henry up once and for all. The 3-D effects
make the horror movie scarier than any I've seen, and
when the face of one of Vincent Price's victims melts, it
seems like it is dripping in my lap. I notice that I'm not
the only one squirming.

Between movies there's a drawing for a prize that
requires the theater's lights be put on. Seeing a movie
house all lit up is kind of strange, and for a minute all

the kids seem to be taking in every part of the large musty auditorium. It's like a mystery is being revealed, and my eyes move across the two balconies and the ornate statues that hang everywhere even at the top of the arch above the stage. I wonder if those particular statues qualify as gargoyles.

A grown-up I assume is the theater's manager or owner because he is in a suit and tie climbs the steps to the stage. He's carrying the box from the lobby in which we all placed our names before the movie. I'm wondering what fortunate kid will be called up on stage to draw the names out of the box. I've never been called on so am totally shocked when I hear my name announced. Fear grips me immediately. The idea of being there in front of hundreds of kids makes my heart pound, and I am anchored to my seat until Corey and Bob practically heave me into the aisle. My legs tremble as I climb the stairs to the stage and cross it to where the manager awaits with the box of names.

"Hiya, David. You want to reach in here and pull out two lucky names?"

I keep my back to the audience as much as possible as I dig two slips of paper from the box.

"Great!" bellows the manager handing me a box of Mike and Ikes for my effort.

I'm dismissed and slink back to my seat as the names on the papers I pluck are read.

"Shhiiit," grumbles Henry, "I never win nothin'. Never even get called up to pick the names. Probably don't let coloreds do that."

"How would he know you're colored until he calls out your name? Then it would be too late for him to change his mind," I reply, and Henry just shrugs and pouts.

All during the second movie he remains silent but on the way out of the theater he announces that he hated "Bwana Devil" because it made coloreds look stupid and helpless.

"No lion will ever eat on me like they did those naked Africans. All they did is wait for the white hunters to save their sad butts. Hate them Tarzan movies, too."

When Corey tells him to lighten up, his response makes us all laugh.

"Don't want to get any lighter 'cause I'll end up looking like you ugly fools."

Our reaction to Henry's remark even tickles him, and by the time we reach the street, he's back to talking about his favorite subject, his cukey.

Before we split up we make plans to gather this coming week at Mr. Brennan's to check on his progress with the boat he's working on to save us from the great hurricane he predicts is coming.

Building the Flo

Mr. Brennan is going to name his boat the Flo after his deceased wife, he announces as Corey, Bob, Henry, and I arrive in his backyard, which is just a half dozen down from mine. The boat looks finished, but Mr. Brennan claims he has a few more things to do before it's seaworthy.

"You got to have a stable rudder or you go where the current takes you, and that can be hazardous to your health, me young mates, he says, sanding a large fin-like piece of wood at his work bench. "The H.M.S. Flo is going to go where I steer her, and I might just steer her to Bermuda some day. Or to that place with those pretty hula-hula gals."

Corey roles his eyes at this statement, and I share some of his skepticism. The Flo does not look as if she is made for the open seas. For one thing it appears top heavy to me because her height is about equal to her length, and I figure that would be a problem in big waves.

"The hurricane season is over, so we got lucky this time. Next year Flo will be ready if the storm tides wash over little Rhody." says Mr. Brennan his eyes drifting skyward.

"How are you going to get the Flo out of your yard, Mr. Brennan?" asks Bob.

"Just got to take that piece of fence over there out of the way and roll her down the driveway hitched to my pickup truck," he replies.

"She gonna' hit them limbs," observes Henry pointing to several drooping branches that form a canopy over the driveway.

"Not after I cut them, sonny," says Mr. Brennan holding up a saw.

"What about them wires?" asks Henry with a challenge in his voice.

"They'll be disconnected and reattached. My friend works for Narragansett Electric, and he'll take care of that for me. Don't you kids worry. I got it all figured out. Just show up when she's ready, and we'll take her down to the bay and go for a sail. You'll be in on her maiden voyage, and that's a very special thing."

We thank Mr. Brennan for including us in this important event. None of us, except Corey, have ever been on a boat before, so he is going to give us some instruction before we launch.

"Everybody can swim, right?" he asks, and only Corey answers in the affirmative.

"Well, that's okay 'cause I got a few Mae West's, and you won't drown with one of them on," says Mr. Brennan digging out several orange life jackets from a locker next to his workbench.

"Bet you kids don't even know who Mae West is," he asks, and Henry says she was that blond lady with big boobaloos in the movies who said sexy things and made all the men drool like hound dogs.

"You got that right. Smart little guy, ain't you?" replies Mr. Brennan with a laugh. "She sure could get you all worked up, that one."

"What if there's a hole in one of those jackets?" asks Bob, his brow furrowed with concern.

"Then you get to sleep at the bottom of the bay with Mae West. Talk about a wet dream. You fellas know what a wet dream is, don't you?" inquires Mr. Brennan his right eyebrow arched.

"It's when your cukey explodes when you've been dreamin' of nudie girls," replies Henry.

"Yeah, I figured you boys would know that one," says Mr. Brennan returning to sanding the rudder.

He has on his "I like Ike" button even though Eisenhower won the election over a year ago. When I point this out, he says, "Ike saved our asses from the Nazis, so I'm going to keep this on in everlasting gratitude."

On our way to the asylum to hang out after stopping by Mr. Brennan's, we debate his qualifications to skipper the Flo, and the consensus is that we better carefully check all the Mae West's for punctures before the boat leaves the shore with us on it.

During the ten minutes it takes us to reach the asylum, thick clouds have formed, and they cast a gloomy shadow over the abandoned building giving it a more foreboding appearance than usual.

"Someday that place is just going to eat us up like the whale did to Jonah," remarks Bob somberly. "Bet it's related to the Polio House," he adds, as we shimmy up the gutter to its boarded entrance.

Shocking Stories

We entertain ourselves in the electro-shock room by telling ghost stories. Corey tells a whopper about his grandparent's house in Alaska. Apparently it was occupied by the spirits of two men who were hung in the backyard of the house after they were accused of killing a prospector during the gold rush. It turns out they were innocent and ever since they have haunted the grounds and rooms of the old place. Things came to a head, says Corey, when his grandmother was chased from the house to the road by one of the ghosts. It was trying to put a noose around her neck but vanished as soon as her feet left the property. There she stood trembling until her husband returned home that evening. It took a lot of coaxing to get her back in the house, and that very night both ghosts visited them while they slept.

Corey's grandfather was the first to wake up and see them standing at the foot of their bed. When he got his courage up, he asked them what they wanted and they replied "justice." By then, Corey's grandmother was awake and gaping at the phantoms. "Justice" they kept repeating and slowly faded away never to be encountered again. That was thirty years ago, and now Corey's grandparents are not entirely convinced any of it ever happened, but they love telling the story when people come to visit them.

"I think I saw them, though, when I first went to Alaska to spend part of my school vacation with my grandparents," reveals Corey. "In the middle of the night I heard some voices outside my bedroom window. What I heard sounded like what my grandpa said the ghosts said to him when they came to his bed. 'Justice . . . justice . . . justice.' When I looked out the window, I saw two big shadows moving across the yard. It was late at night, but it doesn't get dark up there in the summer like it does here. When I heard the voices come out of the Polio House the time I cut through its yard, I got the same creepy feeling. Something dead was talking to me."

"Awful lot a dead folks talkin' to livin' folks, seems to me. Ketch got his little girl ghost in his room, too. Hey, maybe the next time she visits you she'll yank your cukey if you ask her," jokes Henry.

"She's only five years old. At least that's how old she was when she died," I say giving Henry a disapproving look.

"Yeah, but I bet she'll get her tiny hand around what you got, seein' how you ain't got that much," shoots back Henry while striking a match and tossing it in the air like a rocket.

"Hey, you want to set this place on fire? Stop that you little creep," says Corey, grabbing at Henry's book of matches.

Henry is way too fast for Corey and in a split second he disappears into a dark corner of the shock room. We begin to search for him with our flashlights when, suddenly, the room is fully lit up by the flames of an entire book of matches that Henry has ignited and tossed over our heads.

"You goddamn fool! You're going to burn down this place!" shouts Corey. ""Stop it or I'll whip up on you like Rocky Marciano!" he adds waving his fist at Henry.

"Ain't gonna burn down the dump 'cause I got no more matches," replies Henry nonchalantly as we all take turns stamping out the would-be fire.

"Bet you could see this ole place a hundred miles if it was burnin'," says Henry, rejoining us near the shock machine.

His actions have dampened our enthusiasm for hanging out in the asylum, so we exit the building without saying another word to Henry, who remarks that he has discovered a whole new wonderful way to remove the starch from his thing.

"You get some raw liver and wrap it around it. It feels just like pussy," he says, attempting to get back into our good graces.

After awhile Henry goes his own way calling us a bunch of sour farts, and Bob makes the observation that maybe black dwarfs are crazier than most people.

"Maybe having such a big head and little body gets things twisted up," he says, and I reply that there are plenty of sane midgets in the world. "Maybe its because he's colored, too," adds Bob, and we walk home pondering that possibility.

Lick and Stick

Things are not a hundred percent with my mother yet. She is slowly improving but still pretty weak. Mostly she passes the day in the living room rocker reading or sticking S & H Green stamps into their books. She's been collecting them in a large shoebox forever and says this is the perfect opportunity to paste them into the books and redeem them for something nice. She has in mind a big toaster oven that requires bunches of books. Her fingers are sticky from the process and she has resorted to using a wet sponge to glue them into the books because her mouth has run out of spit and her tongue has become cottony, she says, sticking it out as if to prove her point.

My sister and I want a transistor radio, but my mother says we'll have to save up for it ourselves because a roaster oven is a much more useful item since the oven in our stove has become nearly useless and takes forever to cook anything. Linda has collected about a few books of her own stamps, but I have none, so the prospect of my getting a transistor is not great, and if my sister saves up enough for one, I doubt she'll share it with me anyway.

"You could get another job and buy one," says my father, who was not thrilled when I gave up my paper route last Spring because I was tired of combating aggressive dogs in the neighborhood where I made deliveries.

My father had made me a wooden club to use on the hounds instructing me to rap them on the snout when they came after me. The idea of whacking a dog, even if it was about to take a chunk out of my leg, didn't appeal to me because future vets just don't harm animals, so I quit the route, which someone else quickly took and was bitten the first day on the job.

Sympathetic to my situation my mom makes me a deal, which doesn't set well with my sister.

"You help me fill the books and any I have left over after trading them for the roaster oven, I'll give to you," she offers, and I gladly accept.

"Why does he get the extras?" complains Linda as I enthusiastically join my mom pasting the stamps into their books. "I've been saving them and he hasn't been doing anything. All he does is hang out in that old building with his dumb friends. He does other stupid things, too," she says, giving me a threatening look.

"You do some things, too," I say hoping she picks up on my meaning when I stick out my chest and shake it.

My mother misses this gesture but has had enough of our bickering and threatens to lick us instead of the stamps if we don't stop with our nonsense.

"Balls McCarthy! You'd think I'd get a little better behavior from you two after what I've been through," she says dropping the book she is filling onto the floor and climbing from the rocking chair. "Now you can both stamp these books while I get back to my book.

She is reading a book called *The Power of Positive Thinking* that she claims is helping her get better. When she leaves the room, Linda calls me a little piss head and says the next time she's going to blow the whistle on me about drinking wine with my moron friends.

I counter her threat by saying I'll tell our parents about her showing off her naked breast to guys.

"And I'll tell them that your midget friend made it all up. They know he's a liar and creep like your other stupid friends, so they won't believe it."

"He's better than you are," I protest, adding that her snooty friends do things that are a lot worse than what we do.

When my father re-enters the living room, it is obvious that he has gotten an earful about us from his wife, and he is none too happy about it.

"Go ahead, keep acting like this and see where it gets you," is all he has to say before flopping on the couch and burying his face in the newspaper.

For about an hour my sister and I silently stick the little green stamps into the tiny squares in their books, occasionally shooting one another a hostile look. When our mother reappears she has little to say to us, waving us off like we are pesky flying insects buzzing around her head when we ask how she is.

Boxed In

I wake up gasping for air. It's as if someone has been sucking the oxygen from my lungs. I've been dreaming a nightmare. In it Mary Kay does not have polio. She is skipping toward me as I sit on the steps of the porch. She is dressed in her First Communion outfit, and I am both baffled and thrilled by her sudden miraculous recovery. When I rise to enthusiastically greet her, she moves on past me without even acknowledging my presence and continues on to the Polio House across the street. Once there she springs up the steps as the front door swings open and she disappears inside.

I know I have to follow her but the thought of doing it fills me with dread. When I reluctantly approach the house, Mary Kay emerges holding dead Sara by the hand. They wave at me and then from the dark recesses of the house I detect movement. More chills shoot up my back. As Mary Kay and Sara descend the steps her brothers exit the house and are followed by their parents–Mr. and Mrs. Clayburgh. They're dripping wet and covered with long slimy pieces of seaweed.

They are coughing and choking and their eyes are wide with panic and horror as they move toward me. It is then that I wake up coughing and choking, too, like I'm drowning.

The rest of the night I clutch a hold of Topper afraid to move and expecting the whole dead family to appear in my room at any moment. As soon as daybreak arrives I gather my courage to take a long delayed pee out of the window. Then I return to bed and fall into a deep sleep, which is soon interrupted by my mother's voice telling me that it's time to get up even though my alarm clock hasn't sounded. Before I go to school she wants me to pick up something for her at the store.

"Just ask for the brown box," she says, and I tell her to get Linda to go, because I hate getting this for her.

"Linda is already gone. She had a field trip today, so you have to do this for me. You don't have to ask for Kotex. They know what you mean when you ask for the brown box. No one will know what it is you're bringing home. Don't be so silly. Women's periods are a fact of life, and half the people in the world have them. It's nothing to be ashamed about. It's 1954, not the dark ages."

The fact is everybody knows what the brown boxes are, especially my friends and other guys, who I'm certain I'll bump into on my way home. It's just too embarrassing to be seen with a box of Kotex. The store does not put it in a bag because it's already wrapped in brown paper, so you have to carry it home for the whole world to see.

I delay getting dressed as much as I can, thinking that it will be too late for me to run the humiliating errand, but this strategy fails as my mom has shrewdly allowed for extra time by getting me up a half hour earlier than usual. When I check the time on my Baby Ben my heart sinks. On my way out of the house, I run into Corey.

"What are you doing here?" I ask, surprised to see him at this hour, and he says he was up before dawn to see his mom off to the airport because she was assigned an early flight.

"I couldn't get back to sleep, so I figured I'd head to school early and shoot some cards. Why are you out already?" he asks, and I say that I'm on a personal errand for my mother.

"You mean you got to get her the rags, right?" he says matter-of-factly. "No big deal. I'll go with you. I get the stuff for my mom all the time."

I'm relieved that he will accompany me and thrilled when he agrees to purchase the brown box for me. On our way back to my house, we boldly play catch with it.

When we pass Mary Kay's house, her mother is on the porch, and we do our best to hide the box.

"Hi kids. Going to school? It's the other way," she jokes, and we tell her we forgot something at my house and are just returning to get it. "Mary Kay is about ready to go for her walk around the block. She's doing real good."

Corey and I pick up our pace while still doing our best to conceal the Kotex box.

"See you later, David. Mary Kay is looking forward to your visit," she says, and I shout back that I am, too.

A minute later I deliver the package of shame to my mother while Corey waits outside.

"See, that wasn't so hard, was it?" she says, handing me a piece of toast to eat on the way to school.

"No big deal," I say, and rejoin Corey on the porch.

"Somebody should tear down that old place," says Corey pointing to the Polio House. "Nobody would ever live there after what happened."

"Yeah, that would be good" I reply, wondering if that would mean the end of the Clayburgh ghosts, or if they would then take up residence in my attic room once and for all.

The Dare

Bob and Henry are waiting in the schoolyard when we arrive. Again, Henry is all for cutting class, but the vote is split. Bob is for it, but Corey and I point out that since it's only a half-day, due to a teacher's meeting, we should attend and get credit for being there. Our reasoning wins out, but not without the usual ridicule from Henry, which is mostly directed at me.

"You're the biggest chicken, Ketch. Always wantin' to do what your mama wants. 'David, make sure you go to school. David, be a good little boy. David, wipe your hiney,'" he says mockingly in a falsetto voice.

This gets to me, and I launch a counter attack. "Your mom wears combat boots," I retort feebly, but it has the hoped for effect on Henry, who threatens to pop me in the nose if I say another thing about his mama.

"It will take a bigger person than you," I reply not meaning the inadvertent reference to his size.

"I'm gonna' kick your skinny wazoo, boy!" he shouts, his fists clenched and poised to charge at me.

"You and whose army?" I fire back pressing against Corey.

"Clamp it, you guys," says Corey, who wedges his body between us. "We're friends, remember?"

"Ain't a friend of no chicken," says Henry, stepping back and unclenching his balled up hands.

"Who's a chicken?" I reply.

"Well, if you ain't no chicken, I dare you to go into the Polio House by yourself," challenges Henry, with a look of defiance in his large dark eyes.

"Why would I do that?" I answer. "That's stupid."

"See, he's a scaredy baby after all," says Henry triumphantly.

"Okay, I'll go in. No big deal," I say, immediately regretting my words.

The plan is set. After school I'll enter the Polio House through a cellar window. I'll then proceed to the second floor and signal the guys as they watch from the street. Despite my trepidation about the plan I maintain an appearance of nonchalance.

"No big deal," I repeat, and Henry says it will be a big deal when the Clayburghs grab me by the neck and tear me from limb to limb for trespassing on their property.

At noon school lets out and we head to the Polio House. All morning long I have been unable to shake the feeling that what I am about to do is a very bad idea. Stupid me, I think. I get myself into things like this sometimes, and I don't know why.

"So you goin' into the house, or ain't you?" asks Henry as we stand across the street from my date with the damned.

"Yeah, I'm going in, but then you got to go in after I do," I remind Henry, who has agreed to enter the Polio House if I do.

"Don't you worry, boy. I'll be going in to fetch your body," he replies with a wide taunting smile.

Ever the practical one Corey warns me that what I'm about to do is against the law, so I ask him and Bob to watch out for the cops and whistle if they see any. With that I head across the street to greet my fate. My heart is pounding because I suspect dead Sara is waiting for me in the dark recesses of the decaying structure.

I manage to squeeze my body through the small cellar window landing on its cold, damp floor. The light outside seems to stop at the window and it is almost completely dark. I move slowly and cautiously with my arms stretched in front of me to what I vaguely make out to be stairs leading up to the first floor. They creak as I climb them and I expect the door at the top to swing open and the ghoulish spirits of the Clayburgh's to come rushing down on me. When I push against the door it opens without resistance revealing more dark space, which I figure to be the kitchen. Beyond it I detect some light that apparently is seeping through the boards that mostly cover the front room windows. It reminds me of the insides of the asylum, and like a moth I'm drawn to the dull glow. All I have to do is make it to the second floor and wave at my waiting friends to be a hero, but I am not sure that is in the cards because I'm sure something hideous is about to leap at me from any direction.

The living room contains a couch and a chair. Both are on their sides and have large tears in their upholstery.

Stuffing pours from what look like angry slashes made by the machete of a madman . . . a madman waiting to do the same to me. Chills roll up and down my spine in prickly waves as I begin my ascent to the second floor. It is brighter up there because the windows have not been covered with boards, and I feel slight relief as I enter the front bedroom. A mattress is on the floor and there are beer and liquor bottles strewn around it. Someone has been here, I conclude, heading to the window. In addition to the bottles there are a few envelopes and other junk scattered over the floor and a small upturned desk in the corner with its drawers pulled out. More papers flow from them, and I'm suddenly curious why they would be left behind.

When I pick up one of the envelopes to keep as a trophy of my courageous expedition in the unknown, my heart shudders from a noise coming from the hall. My brain says it's Sara and her parents who have come to punish me for entering their tomb.

"David . . . David," murmurs a hollow voice beyond the bedroom door, and I figure I am doomed.

"Who's there?" I manage to gasp as my name continues to be uttered.

Through the ragged lace curtains hanging from the window I can see Corey and Bob, and I consider making a leap for it before I am trapped by the approaching monster, but this won't happen because I have become frozen in place. Suddenly there's a big bang and I cannot keep from letting out a loud pathetic scream when a shadowy object comes flying into the room. It's Henry and he falls onto the mattress in hysterics.

"Bet you crapped your drawers," Ketch," he manages to say between fits of laughter, and I want to choke him. Instead I stomp out of the room and make my way for the cellar exit.

"David . . . Oh, David," he bellows as I make my way downstairs. "David, it's Sara. I want to yank your lil' white boy cukey."

A Break

I have had my fill of the guys, for a while at least, so today I plan to spend time with Mary Kay. We're going for a long walk or for one as long as she can handle. My mom is not feeling up to par, she says, and wants my sister and me to help her clean the house before I go to Mary Kay's. Linda declares the vacuuming as her contribution, and I offer to wash and wax the kitchen floor, something I have done before and don't really mind doing. This is fine with my mom, who claims that her energy level is still way off compared to where it was before she got polio.

"I don't know if I'll ever be my old self again," she says flopping onto the couch, and my dad reminds her that it's only been a short time since she was sick.

"Jesus, you had polio for God's sake. What do you expect? What about all that positive thinking you've been raving about?" he asks, irritated with her impatience.

He has stuck to his vow not to drink beer again, but it has made him crabby and jumpy. His view of the decline of the neighborhood has become darker, and he predicts it will soon be made into a slum because of more colored people moving in. He continues to complain about the old Clayburgh house, too, saying it only makes matters worse because of its falling down condition.

"It's like a welcome sign to all the coloreds that this is their kind of neighborhood. It makes everything around it look worse," he complains shaking his head is disgust.

The ghosts might have something to say about anybody getting rid of it, I venture, and my dad tells me not to start on that stupid line of thought. My sister agrees with him, saying I have bats in my belfry.

"Don't listen to him, daddy. Him and his dumb friends love to make up stories. They're so immature."

"What about your stupid boyfriends," I reply threateningly, and Linda tells me to shut up and mind my own business.

"Both of you shut up and go do your chores. You're giving your mother a pain in the butt on top of the headache she already has," barks my dad.

After I coat the kitchen floor with wax, Topper comes tromping across it, and I have to do it again. When I'm sure it's dry I head out to Mary Kay's. She's waiting expectantly on the porch of her house, and as soon as she spots me, she rises from her wheel chair clutching her wooden crutches. She beams at me as I stride up the steps two at a time.

"I'm ready for our walk," she says, and her mother emerges from the house.

"Maybe I should come with you, honey," she says apprehensively. "You're still a little shaky, and David hasn't walked with you before. It's a big responsibility for him."

"Please, mother. We'll be okay," Mary Kay responds and moves to the top of the steps.

"Well, I can at least help you down to the sidewalk, sweetie. Keep a close eye on her, David. She thinks she's ready to run a race," says Mrs. Walton, and I agree to watch her like a hawk.

Getting down the steps is not an easy feat for poor Mary Kay, even with two people helping her. On the sidewalk, everyone breathes a sigh of relief and Mary Kay lets out a hooray. It's the first time she'll be walking without the accompaniment of her mom, and this obviously is a momentous breakthrough for her.

Her mother reluctantly returns to the porch, the whole while keeping a wary eye on us as we move slowly down the street.

"Don't try to do too much, Mary Kay!" shouts her mother, and I wave acknowledgment.

Mary Kay's movements are jerky and tentative, and I fear that at any moment she may topple to the pavement. However, her steely determination puts her in good stead and she remains upright and moving in baby steps down the block.

"I think I could walk to school," she announces, and I think that would take us the remainder of the afternoon at the speed we are going. "But I won't do it this time. Maybe soon though, if you'll come with me."

"Of course, I will," I say, adding that we could walk to Mr. Brennan's house for the launch of his boat, because he's only a short distance away.

"He's gonna move his boat out of his yard any day now and take it down to the bay for its maiden voyage. He wants us to go with him."

"I really can't," she says, disappointment replacing her smile.

"Don't tell your mom. We could say we're just going to watch Mr. Brennan work on his boat. He's going to hook it up to his truck and drop it in the water close by before the weather gets too bad. Then we'll take it for a cruise and come right back. It's going to be great."

"I couldn't lie to my mother," replies Mary Kay, looking somber.

"It's just a white lie. You're really telling her the truth . . . mostly. You're going to Mr. Brennan's to watch him work on his boat, and that's what you're doing."

"I'll think about it, Ketch," says Mary Kay as we come to the end of the block. "Look, I've walked almost a whole block on my own. Let's do some more, okay?"

"Sure," I say, wondering how fast she can move across the street where cars are known to travel many miles over the speed limit.

On the other side, Mary Kay's enthusiasm reaches another high, and she can't keep from reaching out and squeezing my arm. She's staring at me and there is nothing but joy in her eyes. This is love. I could propose to her right now.

"I like you a lot," I say to her. To me, it's the closest thing to a marriage proposal. She replies that I am her best friend, "in the whole world."

Boil Man

My resolve to steer clear of my buddies lasts until Sunday afternoon when Corey and Bob show up at my house. Henry is not with them, and I'm glad for that. I am still peeved at him over the Polio House business, so I would like to put a couple of more days between us, although that will not be easy because I know I will see him at school if he doesn't play hooky.

Bob suggests we go down to the bus station to see a guy he calls the Boil Man. Apparently the baggage clerk at the Greyhound is covered from head to toe with millions of lumps resembling boils, and Bob is totally intrigued by him.

"You got to see this guy. It's creepy. He's got them every where, even in his ears," says Bob, and we decide to go check him out.

Sure enough, as soon as we enter the bus depot we spot him carrying luggage out to a waiting bus. We move toward him for a closer look all the while trying not to be too obvious about it. Every inch of his visible skin is covered with ugly knobs, some quite large. One of his eyes is even partially blocked by a fleshy nugget. It is a horrendous sight, and I am at once repulsed by his appearance and sympathetic for the misery it must cause him. Lately I've been getting some pretty big pimples, and I wonder if it could ever lead to that.

"He probably has them on his dick," comments Corey, and Bob adds that he probably has them on his gonads, too.

His grim condition inspires all sorts of speculation, which we entertain as we watch him load luggage in the baggage compartment under the bus.

"You think he feels them when he goes to bed? It must be like sleeping on a pile of gravel," says Bob.

"Wonder if he had them when he was a kid? Maybe his parents had them too," comments Corey.

"Maybe they get full of puss and they pop," I speculate while running my finger over a pimple that has recently burst through the skin over my right eye. "I'd cut them off, if I had them," I continue, and Corey says I'd have to skin my entire body to get rid of what he has.

"He could get a better job with a circus freak show, I bet," says Bob. That's what I'd do. Be more fun than loading suitcases, and you'd get to travel a lot and hump the bearded lady."

"I don't think anyone would do it with him. Not even the bearded lady," says Corey, his eyes fixed on the deformed baggage handler.

"What a crummy way to live," observes Bob becoming serious. "I'd kill myself."

Corey and I agree that we would probably end it, too, and with that we decide to leave the domain of the Boil

Man in preference of smooth skinned Mr. Brennan's house.

"You think he ever forgets about all those lumps?" asks Bob.

"Would you?" replies Corey, and Bob shakes his head no.

"I'd cover every mirror in my house," I say, and Bob repeats that he would just end it.

"Life must stink for him, so why bother?" he says, as we head out of the depot and begin our trek back to South Providence.

"Wonder where he lives?" I speculate, adding, "Maybe he lives in the sewers or in a cave somewhere."

"Doubt that," replies Corey, who then announces he may be moving away because his mother is seriously thinking about a reassignment to Australia by the airline she is working for because it pays a lot better.

"Australia is on the other side of the planet. What's there? I mean, anything besides kangaroos?" asks Bob.

"I don't want to go, but my mom says we'd be living in a real nice place in Sydney. It's a big city, she says, like Boston," observes Corey.

"Hey, can I come with you? I'd love to get away from here. I could get a job," asks Bob, and Corey says he doubts it.

I'm shocked. It has never occurred to me that any of my friends would move away.

"You're really going to move?" I ask Corey, and he says his mom is thinking about it, but he believes it is likely.

"When?" I ask, and he says within the next year or maybe sooner.

This drives my mood downward, and by the time we reach Mr. Brennan's place, I can hardly speak. Bob continues to inquire about the possibility of moving to Australia with Corey, who tries to discourage him of the notion.

"Hi fellas'," says the skipper of the Flo when we reach his backyard. "What do you think?" he asks, pointing the paintbrush in his hand at the boat. "You like the color?"

The underside of the boat is a bright red, and we're told that when it dries the Flo will be ready to take her first cruise. Sometime next week, Mr. Brennan estimates.

"You greenhorns gonna' be ready? Where's your little colored friend? Want him to come along for luck. God watches out for the less fortunate, and he sure appears less fortunate. We won't sink with him on board," he laughs, and we say we'll bring him along.

"Can Mary Kay come?" I ask, and Mr. Brennan says with a gimp on board, too, we could weather a typhoon.

While Bob chuckles, I fail to see the humor in his reference to Mary Kay as a gimp and feel anger welling up in me.

"Well, you guys be here early next Wednesday. That's when we're going to ship out," say Mr. Brennan, turning his back on us and applying his brush to a spot on the bottom of the boat he has missed. "Now get along, swabbies. I got work to do here afore we set sail."

On our way out of the yard, Bob says maybe we could all sail to Australia on the Flo, and Corey observes that he doubts the tub would reach much beyond Block Island, only a few miles off the Rhode Island coast.

The Flo Floats

My dad has broken his promise not to drink beer. He tells me to keep quiet about it when I catch him taking a deep swig from a Narragansett Beer bottle while sitting on the back door steps.

"Say nothing to your mom, okay? After this one, I'll stop. Just needed a break, and this was in the refrigerator getting very lonely."

He seems even gloomier than usual, and when I ask what's bothering him, he looks at me straight on and says *life.*

"So, you been seeing anymore ghosts lately, Davy?" he asks changing the subject and looking back at his beer bottle.

I report that I do hear noises coming from the Polio House sometimes late at night, and he says the place is a misery to everyone.

"Don't know why the city doesn't condemn the dump. I'd gladly help take it down."

"Maybe someone will buy it and fix it up," I offer, and he says that the place is way beyond saving.

"It's going to just crumble in a heap one of these days. It would take a fortune to get it in shape to live in and nobody's going to spend that kind of dough in this neighborhood. The roof's shot for one thing, and the place would have to be re-shingled, too. Can only imagine what the joint looks like inside."

I'm about to comment about it being pretty okay inside when I catch myself figuring he would be really pissed off if he knew I had been in there.

"It might be better inside than outside," I offer, and he says he seriously doubts it before swallowing the remainder of his beer.

"Well, who knows? Maybe something will change the situation," he says, tossing the empty bottle into the trash bucket and heading back into the house.

When Wednesday rolls around, we all head to Mr. Brennan's for the launch of the Flo. Mary Kay has come down with a cold, so she can't accompany us, not that she would have anyway. I have mended things with Henry, so he joins Bob, Corey, and me.

"You sure this thing's gonna' float? I can't swim so you're gonna' have to fish me out if it sinks," he says directing his comments to Corey, who he assumes could save us all if the Flo goes down on her trial run.

"I can't swim either," admits Corey and Henry expresses serious second thoughts about coming with us.

"Shhiiiit! I'm too young and good lookin' to die. Maybe I'll just watch you fools from the shore," he says as we enter Mr. Brennan's cluttered yard.

He's waiting for us and has already hooked up the trailer holding the Flo to his old truck. The canopy of tree limbs over the driveway has been dramatically cut back and the wires crossing it have been removed.

"I can ride a couple of you sailors in the truck. The rest of you have to ride in the back or in the boat," he says, and Corey and Bob quickly volunteer to ride in the boat.

"Maybe it would be better if the little colored guy and Bob ride in the boat since they're the smallest," observes Mr. Brennan, and both Bob and Henry eagerly hop onto the Flo.

It takes about twenty minutes to locate Mr. Brennan's special place along the shore of the bay to launch the Flo. He backs the truck to a point to where the trailer is submerged in the murky water, and he unhooks the boat. After he parks the truck up the shore a couple hundred feet, he lifts himself aboard Flo where we already await him. He then takes a miniature bottle of liquor, what I've heard my dad call cordials, out of his jacket pocket and gently taps it against the boat's bright red hull.

"I christen thee the H.M.S. Flo," he announces grandly and then uncaps the unbroken bottle and chugs its contents and does the same with another tiny bottle of booze.

He then takes a small American flag out of a metal box and attaches it to a flag pole at the rear of the boat.

"Okay, you swabs, let's say the Pledge of Allegiance before we set sail," he says leading us in the pledge.

Henry rolls his eyes and salutes with his middle finger during the ceremony. Mr. Brennan is oblivious to his ornery behavior, and the rest of us do our best to ignore him, too. Being disrespectful to the flag is not something any of us find funny, and halfway through the pledge Henry picks up on our disapproval and gives the flag a full-fingered salute, too.

"Anchors away!" shouts Mr. Brennan, pulling the rope from the small outboard motor, and we are moving out into the harbor. "We have a mission to complete," he adds, and we ask what that is besides christening the Flo.

"We're gonna' locate the wreck," he answers, and we ask what wreck. "The Clayburgh's boat, me laddies" he says, and we stare at each other in total surprise. "They called their skiff Sara, after their little girl. Figure they went down around Prudence Island, the way the tides are. We'll go take a look-see, okay? Won't take all that long. We're riding the tide, so we'll gain some knots. Be back in a couple of hours. In the meantime, which one of you sailors wants to take the helm?"

Henry leaps to his feet, waving his hand, but Mr. Brennan acts like he doesn't see him, and offers the wheel to Corey. Henry looks disappointed and angry as Mr. Brennan directs Corey on how to keep the boat headed to the potential site of the Sara.

"You got port side over there and starboard side over there. You turn the wheel one full turn when I say 'one point off the starboard bow' or 'one point off the port bow' and two full turns if I say 'two points,'" instructs Mr. Brennan.

The Flo moves across the water at a greater speed than we imagined it capable of, and we're all truly enjoying the experience, all except Henry, who crouches in the corner of the small deck pouting and igniting matches one after another and tossing them overboard. This earns him a stern scolding from Mr. Brennan.

"Hey, don't do that, you crazy little nig . . . jerk," he bellows, catching himself before calling Henry the worse name. "You can blow us to smithereens. There's gasoline fumes all over the place."

Henry gives Mr. Brennan a hard look of defiance but tosses the remaining matches into the dark green water.

"How we gonna' blow up with all this water out here?" he asks in a challenging tone.

"You nuts, boy? Ships blow up all the time because of fires. That's how most of 'em go down. They burn away on top of the water and then sink. Didn't make the Flo for that awful fate. So you keep the fire in your britches. Hear?"

Henry begrudgingly agrees to Mr. Brennan's demand, and a few minutes later confides to me that he thinks the skipper is related to Bob's crazy mother, and he figures we will be lucky it we don't end up at the bottom of the sea like the Clayburgh's.

"He's a loony ole bird," whispers Henry, into my ear, and when I shoosh him, he says that I am nuts, too, his voice rising. "Guess I'll be in some kinda' sad place out here in all this ocean with nothin' but silly ass white boys who're crazy on top of everythin' else."

Mr. Brennan overhears Henry's comments and half-jokingly remarks he has heard that people with dark skin sink to the bottom twice as fast as those with light skin, and he may be inclined to test this theory on Henry if he does not stop his foolish prattle. This halts the flow of venom from Henry's mouth but not for long.

Sighting Sara

About an hour after launch we approach Prudence Island. It is a lonely and desolate looking place, and as we near it, I have a sense of foreboding, as if something evil is hiding in the thick brush that reaches the water's edge.

"We're gonna' schooner 'round the inlets a little. Have a hunch we might just find something. The island is kind of a catch basin for everything that floats down from town," says Mr. Brennan directing the boat closer to the island.

Henry has not said a word since his rebuke by Mr. Brennan and Corey and Bob are just enjoying the whole experience as their bare feet dangle from the side of the boat. For late-October it feels like summer, and I think that if any of us could swim we probably would already have done so.

"There's a good spot to check out," says Mr. Brennan rotating the helm to glide us into a small depression in the coastline.

Mr. Brennan instructs us to keep our eyes peeled for anything that looks suspicious, like pieces of wood or any objects that appear like they came from a boat wreck. For several minutes we scour the shoreline of the inlet but make no sightings of an unusual nature.

"There's a bunch of these, so let's head on to the next one. Just up the way."

The results of our search are the same as we cruise the next two inlets, but in the third we notice an object protruding from the high grass along the shore.

"Stand to, mates," shouts Mr. Brennan, and we approach what looks like a piece of wood painted blue.

Mr. Brennan extends a long hook and snags the object, hauling it to the boat.

"It's something. Definitely a piece of boat," says Mr. Brennan exuberantly. "Here, Corey, grab it and haul it on board."

Without breaking a sweat, Corey lifts the object from the water and plunks it down on the deck.

"It's just junk," says Henry, breaking his long silence, and Mr. Brennan says perhaps but it may be junk with a story.

"Sometimes you got to look below the surfaces of things to find the answer you're looking for, sonny," says Mr. Brennan closely inspecting the two-foot piece of wood.

After a few seconds a large smile spreads across his weathered face, and he points to something on the retrieved hunk of wood. There before us is the better part of the letter "S," which immediately gives me the shivers.

"Well, mates, I believe we've located the ghost boat.

"How do you know that?" spouts Henry cynically.

"Well, the Clayburgh's boat was called Sara, right?" asks Mr. Brennan, and we all acknowledge that fact. "She was also painted blue," he adds, and our skepticism starts to erode.

We spend several minutes searching the area for what Mr. Brennan calls further evidence, but we come up empty handed. As we are leaving the inlet to head back home, I notice something moving in the high grass, and for a split second I'm convinced it is the ghost that has taken to haunting me in my bedroom.

Another Discovery

Mr. Brennan says he will take the piece of wood to the police in the hope they will launch a full-scale search of the Prudence Island area for the rest of the Sara and her unfortunate passengers.   He is all charged up by the discovery and in his enthusiasm shares the contents of a bottle of Southern Comfort he has been sipping from since we started sailing home.   This quickly puts us all in an elevated mood and we belt out "99 Bottles of Beer" as we cruise back to Providence.

Suddenly Mr. Brennan says, "I killed my Flo."

His face is sharp and frozen.   None of us says a word.

"See, I told you he's crazy," Henry whispers in my ear.

"I had to," Mr. Brennan says.   "She was suffering from the cancer and in horrible pain.   Gilly, please stop the hurt, she'd plead.   I loved my Flo, so I had to help her.   What else could I do?   So I put a pillow over her sweet face while she was sleeping, and she didn't hurt no more. Didn't even move. No struggle at all. Not even a whisper. It was like she was making it easy for me."

"You be funning us," Henry says, and we all laugh short laughs to see what Mr. Brennan says next. I am hoping he will start to laugh, too.

"She was all I had, and there she was all withered up in hurt and crying 'Help me, Gilly. Help me.' So I did. Police figured she died of natural causes. Cancer ain't natural though. Nothing that eats you up inside is natural. You put a dog down when it's hurtin'. Why not a person you love? Cruel not to."

Mr. Brennan slumps to the deck, and Corey takes the helm, aiming the boat in the direction of the spot where we launched the Flo. In a few minutes Mr. Brennan is out cold and snoring loudly, and we're left to navigate back home.

"He's a murderer," says Henry, and Bob tells him to shut up, that someone should have done the same to his mom.

"We can't report him," I say, and everyone agrees, including Henry.

"Yeah, he'd be sent to the 'lectric chair for sure."

"Don't say nothing to nobody," says Bob, adding "Mr. Brennan ain't no murderer. You're not a murderer if you kill someone who wants you to, someone who is dying anyway."

We all accept this point of view and vow never to say anything about Mr. Brennan's confession to a living soul, not even our parents. It has been a day of eerie revelations, and it has left us feeling more connected to one another and older and wiser than when we set out on the Flo's maiden voyage.

Mean Encounter

For several days after returning to shore we're not sure what to do. Whether to stick to our promise about saying nothing about Mr. Brennan killing his sick wife or go to the police and report it. What's more we're not certain he wasn't making up a story because he was half in the bag. Again we resolve to say nothing. If it did happen, it was an act of kindness, we figure, and it would be cruel for Mr. Brennan to go to jail for ending his wife's awful pain.

The piece of wood from the Sara was turned over to the authorities, says Mr. Brennan, but he doubts they will do anything, as they didn't seem all that interested in the evidence of the Clayburgh's fate.

"They said they'd go look, but I think they have other things to worry about now. It's been nearly two years, and they can't be bothered by something like this. They don't suspect foul play. At worst a tragic accident, so maybe they'll go look and maybe they won't. We did our job, mates, and that's all anyone can do, right? Next week I might just head back out there to see if I can find anything else. You fellas are welcome to come along. Say middle of next week? If you can, come by early, and we'll spend the day," says Mr. Brennan, but we show little interest in the offer, and he does not press us for an answer.

Later when the subject comes up on our way home we all agree that we should steer clear of Mr. Brennan for a while. We're also surprised he has said nothing about his startling confession, which makes us think he was just saying something crazy because he was drunk or can't remember.

"He's pretty weird, don't you think?" remarks Henry, and Corey says he thinks Mr. Brennan is basically all right, just not as sane or normal as most people.

"Bet it made him really sad about what he had to do to his wife. He probably hasn't been rowing with both oars since," quips Corey.

"Yeah," agrees Bob, adding "He just wants to help out the poor Clayburgh family to make him feel better about things. Got all that guilt inside."

"You think he's sorry he told us about killing Mrs. Brennan?" I ask, and Henry says that it may bring out the real murderer in him and that he'll probably try to kill us all if we go back out to look for the Clayburgh's boat.

"Well. I ain't tempting fate," says Corey, and we all nix the idea of accompanying Mr. Brennan to the Prudence Island wreck site next week, all except Bob, that is.

"He's okay. We should go with him. I think I will."

Corey says he's got to get home quickly, so he's going to run the rest of the way, and Bob says he's going back to Mr. Brennan's house to see if he has any more booze he'd like to share.

"You're one silly boy," remarks Henry about Bob's intention, and with that the two of us head over to Mary Kay's house to give her a full report on our high sea adventure.

On our way, a car with older teenagers slows to within a few feet of us, and one of the occupants calls to us.

"Hey, you squirts, want a ride?"

We know it is not a genuine offer because these are the same greasers who taunted us a few weeks ago when we had on our jackets with the Gargoyle name sewn on them by Mary Kay's mom. They had called us girls and asked if we were going to cheerleader practice for homos.

"Why you hanging out with that nigger midget," shouts another punk from the car, and I see Henry tense up.

"Don't do anything," I tell him, fearing he may worsen an already dangerous situation.

"Hey, little darky, you want to shine my shoes?" says one of the teens in the back seat of the car, and they all laugh.

"You better get home to your mammy. She already sucked us with her big old liver lips," spits out his friend in the front seat.

I sense Henry is about to explode, and I grab his arm and direct him up the stairs of a strange house hoping our antagonists will speed away when they think we're home. To our relief they do just that and we back peddle down the few steps we have climbed.

"I'm gonna kill them the next time I see them," says Henry fighting back tears. "Maybe throw a match in their car next time I see it parked someplace."

"Forget about those jerks," I tell him, and he says that he'll never forget about them.

"Maybe I'll get my uncle's to kick their ass," he says, catching the tears with the palm of his hands as they are about to roll down his face.

"Not all white people are like that," I say offering myself as proof.

"All white people think black skin is ugly and nasty as shit," says Henry, his eyes hardening and now absent of tears.

"Your papa thinks so, too. That's why I ain't never comin' in your dumb ole house again. Ain't bein' with no white folk no more."

"I'd rather be you than the Boil Man down at the bus station," I say before realizing how stupid it is to make such a comparison. "Besides, my dad doesn't hate you," I add trying to distract him from my foolish statement.

My attempt to reassure him that my father actually likes him and thinks he's a funny kid doesn't have the hoped for effect, and he heads off in the opposite direction saying he wants to be alone with his nigger self. It is the first time I have heard him refer to himself in such a way and it's kind of a shock.

"Watch out for those punks in the car," I yell after him, and he just waves me off like what I've said is of no consequence to him.

Two Steps Back

Mrs. Walton has a solemn look on her face when I arrive at Mary Kay's, and I know something's not right.

"Oh Davy, after that long walk she took with you, she hasn't been able to stand. I told her not to overdo it. The doctor says this is a common side effect of the polio and that she'll regain her strength in her legs soon. It's usually a temporary thing, a little set back, but everything will be all right . . . I'm sure," she says straining to smile.

She suggests I wait while she sees if Mary Kay is awake and would like a visitor. While I wait on the porch the hot rod containing the teens that had mouthed off to Henry and me moments earlier cruises by and I make myself invisible. They're traveling in the direction that Henry headed in and I wonder if he's in danger. When the car is halfway down the block I descend the porch steps to the side walk to see if Henry is anywhere in sight. To my relief he is not, and when the greasers take a right turn, I figure Henry is out of harm's way, at least for the time being.

"Come in, David," says Mrs. Walton clutching a large piece of fabric she's apparently sewing. "She wants to see you."

Mary Kay greets me with a faint smile when I enter her room. She's reclined on her bed surrounded by puzzle pieces and her braces are removed revealing her emaciated legs. When she catches me staring at them she quickly covers them with a blanket.

"We went out on Mr. Brennan's boat," I inform her to break the awkwardness of the moment.

"I wish I could have gone with you, but I've been feeling weak the last few days. I got a cold but then my legs started losing their strength. The doctor says that happens when you've had polio, but he says I'll get strong again soon."

"Sure you will, and we can go out on Mr. Brennan's boat then," I say reassuringly.

"What was it like? Was it fun? Did you go far?" asks Mary Kay, the shine returning to her eyes.

"Yeah, it was fun, but nothing really happened. Almost nothing, I mean. We just floated around for a while," I answer while resisting the urge to give her a full account of the eventful day cruising the bay on the Flo.

"Did you see any big fish? Were there lots of waves?" asks Mary Kay, hungry for a description of the outing.

"We really didn't see much of anything, and it was very calm. No waves or anything," I reply detecting the disappointment in her eyes. "But we did find a piece of the Clayburgh's boat floating around an island, and Mr. Brennan turned it over to the cops."

"Wow, was it really from their boat? That means it sank, right?" asks Mary Kay, now beaming with excitement.

"Yeah, probably . . . or maybe," I say and also reveal that Mr. Brennan shared his whiskey with us on the way back. "We all got a little drunk," I add, catching myself before I say anything about his murdering his wife.

The brightness covering her face suddenly vanishes and she appears on the verge of tears. When I ask what's the matter she covers her face with the sheet and lets out a muffled sob. I'm at a loss for what to do next, and for several moments I just sit and wait as her crying runs its course.

"I . . . I just wish I never got polio. Then I could be normal and have fun like other kids," she says, removing the sheet from her face. "Maybe I'll never be able to do things like everyone else. I'll always be in this bed and that stupid wheelchair."

"Don't be crazy. You're getting better and soon you'll be just like you were before you got sick," I say, and she says that she doubts that, her eyes falling to her legs.

"Some people never get better. They just stay crippled and sick forever."

"Not you," I argue. "Look, you already walk a long way without any help, and when you get over your cold you'll be walking even further."

"Maybe," says Mary Kay, wiping the remaining tears from her eyes. "You're such a good friend, Ketch. I love you, er . . . I mean I like you."

"Me, too," I say, wondering if I should kiss her and ask if she'll marry me someday but instead I just pat her on the shoulder.

"You know what?" says Mary Kay perking up, "I had a dream last night about the little Clayburgh girl, Sara. You were in it, too. She had braces on her legs, too, and you were helping her onto Mr. Brennan's boat. Then she was floating out in the water by herself and crying. I woke up then. That was it, but it seemed real sad and kind of spooky."

When I confess to Mary Kay that I thought I saw her in the high grass near the shore of the island where we found the chunk of wood from the Clayburgh's boat, she says she believes in ghosts.

"I think when something bad happens to people and they die, they remain on earth to haunt the people and places where they once lived. It's like they can't let go and move on to heaven. Do you believe in ghosts, Ketch?"

"Yes," I say, "Pretty much."

The Letter

Despite the dropping temperature, my dad is sitting on our porch when I get home. He grunts a hello as I open the screen door, but his eyes stay fixed on the Polio House. Two empty Narragansett beer bottles rest next to his chair indicating that he's been out on the porch for a while. When I remark that I thought he wasn't going to drink anymore, he says to mind my own business and that he'll drink whatever the hell he wants.

"Fine. Who cares?" I say as I enter the front door of the house where I encounter my sister who is on her way out.

"Hello, little brother. You better see mom. She's really pissed at you," she announces with a smirk.

"Why?" I ask, and she says a truant officer came by today.

"So you and your friends are in big trouble, jerk," she says clearly relishing my predicament.

"Drop dead," I say and head to the kitchen to face the music.

At first my mother ignores the fact that I'm in her presence but then she gives me a hard look and I know harsh words are about to follow.

"I had a visitor today," she says, plopping down into a chair and signaling for me to do the same. "A truant officer. Why have you been playing hooky? You always do so well in school. What's going on with you? He said you missed school the week before last and were seen near that old asylum building over on Paterson Avenue.

It suddenly occurs to me we forgot to have Corey write excuses for that day. Before I can devise an explanation she offers up her thoughts on my truancy.

"It's that Henry boy and your other friends. They're a bad influence on you. That's what I think. Maybe their parents don't care if they go to school, but yours do. We want something more for you than what we've had to do to make a living, but it takes an education. Maybe college, too. You'll never get any where in life without schooling. Your father wasn't as lucky as you. He had to drop out of school to help support his family."

"Does dad know about the truant officer?" I ask, and my mom says she didn't have the heart to tell him, but that if I continue to cut school she will have no choice.

"I promise not to play hooky any more," I say, looking appropriately contrite and feeling sad that I've upset her.

"Don't be influenced by the bad behavior of others. It will get you no place in life, let me tell you," she says, her expression softening.

"My friends didn't force me to play hooky. They're not like that," I offer in their defense.

"The truant officer says they've been missing school, too, so I think you boys are a bad combination, but I'm not going to make you stay away from them. You have to make good judgments on your own, and no one's to blame for what you do but you. Remember that."

"I will," I say and leave the kitchen after planting a conciliatory kiss on her forehead.

"Next time, I'll tell your father, I promise. No more hooky, I mean it. I want you to be something."

As soon as I get to my room, I remember the letter I had taken during my dare into the Polio House. I had stashed it in the bottom drawer of my desk and forgotten it and now, out of nowhere, the urge to read its contents is overwhelming. What secrets does it hold? Does it reveal what happened to the Clayburghs? Why were letters left there when most everything else, except some old rotting furniture, had been removed? Maybe they didn't want to remember the past, when things were better for them. Could be they just wanted to forget everything and leave all the pain and trouble behind, I speculate.

The beat of my heart quickens as I open the soiled white envelope. Doubt and anxiety take hold of me as my sweaty hands unfold the envelope's contents. Had I violated the law by taking the letter? Would I unleash the fury of the dead family for snooping into their private lives?

In the twilight seeping between the dungarees and flannel shirt I have hanging on my bedroom window, I read the letter's content.

My *Dearest Marti,*

I know how difficult this is for you, but there is another way. You have said a thousand times that you no longer can stand things as they are. Now is your chance to change your life. You can, you know. Will you?

In love there is hope!

S.

Who was the Marti the letter addressed, and who was "S?" Sam, Scott, Steve? Or was it a women's initial? Not Sara. Why would she write such a letter? Besides she was too young to even scribble her name when she died. Maybe Shirley or Susan. Maybe Marti was a man's name spelled with an "i" instead of a "y." Probably the only answers to these questions existed in the other papers in the second floor bedroom of the Polio House, and as far as I was concerned nothing was worth reentering that crypt again. This mystery could remain a mystery forever for all I cared.

Mr. Brennan's Theory

"Maybe a boyfriend, but that's pretty hard to fathom. That was Martina's nickname. Everybody called her Marti, but I don't have a clue who the "S" belongs to. Let me see now. About the only guy in this neighborhood whose first name begins with an s is Sully McManus over near Elmwood Avenue, but he's older than I am and even uglier. Marti was a pretty handsome women, so she could have done a lot better than that old dog," says Mr. Brennan chuckling while closely examining the Polio House letter.

"Flo used to hang out with Marti. In fact, they were pretty good friends, that is, till all the trouble broke out. She would take care of the Clayburgh kids sometimes, but when they got the polio, that was it. No way we were gonna' expose ourselves to that. Then Flo fell sick from the cancer, so I guess it didn't matter anyway," continues Mr. Brennan now holding the letter up to the light and checking it out like Sherlock Holmes with a large magnifying glass.

"Good stationary. Not the cheap stuff. So her boyfriend must have had a few bucks."

For several minutes, we both inspect the letter for any other clues it might reveal and then suddenly Mr. Brennan's eyes widen and his posture stiffens.

"Good god almighty. Maybe . . ." he says, and then shakes his head as if to dispel an outrageous thought.

"Maybe what?" I ask, pleading with him to continue.

"Maybe Cal found out," he says, his gaze shifting upward and his hand clenching his jaw.

"Found out what?" I ask, my insides tightening with excitement.

"About Marti's boyfriend, that is if she had one, which I doubt," says Mr. Brennan, returning his gaze toward me. "He was a strong willed man, that Cal, and he wouldn't have taken to that news with a smile. You can bet your month's wages on that, I can tell you."

"What would he have done?"

"Not something pretty. He loved those crippled kids of his, but if he found out Marti was carrying on I think he would have gone crackers. Maybe drown them all and himself too," says Brennan, and the dots begin to connect in my mind.

"Think he took them all out on the boat and sunk it?" I ask, and Mr. Brennan says he figures that could have happened.

"Should we go to the police?"

"It's only a theory, and the cops would probably laugh at us. Then they'd want to know where we got this letter. Get my drift, son?" says Mr. Brennan, and I see where he is heading.

"So what do we do?" I ask, feeling the need to take some form of action.

"Ain't nothing we can do without getting into trouble. Best thing is to forget about it. Remember, it's only a theory. Maybe this "S" person was just a good friend or relative, but I kinda' doubt it."

At one point during the evening that follows I consider reentering the Polio House if Corey and Bob will come along to get more evidence to help prove Mr. Brennan's theory, but then I remember his point about being in illegal possession of property belonging to the Clayburghs.

As I slip into bed I fear that this will be another night of unwelcome visitations, which I really hope stay in my dreams and not actually enter the real world of my frosty loft. Even though Topper is letting loose a steady stream of smelly farts, his big body sprawled over most of the mattress is reassuring. I think of him as my protector against the unknown, although he never acts like something dangerous is close by like I do. Still his being here helps me get to sleep even if he doesn't respond to ghosts.

Dwadillypod

The day after Thanksgiving things erupt at Bob's house. Corey gives me the full account when he comes by later in the day. Bob is missing and his mother is back in the loony bin, he says.

"She went wacky and I guess that started a fight between Bob and his brother. That's what Mark says anyway, but he's a stupid liar. He has bandages around his knuckles, so I think he probably beat the crap out of Bob."

We decide that we have to find Bob, and it occurs to us to check the asylum, and if he is not there to check the roof of the Biltmore.

We come up empty at the asylum after checking the shock room and the other places we hang out there. Marching up and down the dark hallways with our flashlights, we shout Bob's name but get no response. Satisfied that he is nowhere in the abandoned building we head on down to the Biltmore roof.

The sixteen-story climb nearly does us in because our stomachs are still heavy from the day's intake of leftover turkey, and we take a breather on the top floor landing before entering the roof.

"Turkey makes you want to sleep," observes Corey, and I figure that's why we're more pooped than usual.

"If he's not here, god knows where he is," says Corey, and we push open the rooftop door.

Immediately we spot Bob standing on the ledge of the roof with his arms outstretched from his sides. He reminds me of the saint on top of a mountain in some South American city I recently saw in a *National Geographic* magazine.

"Stop!" he shouts. "You come any closer and I'm gonna' jump right now. Screw everything! I mean it. Don't get any nearer."

Even from our distant vantage point, we can see that there is blood on his face and that his shirt is torn.

"Lousy life. I hate it! Crazy mom and stinking brother always picking on me. Better off dead than living with that crummy family."

"You're our friend, Bob. Please come down," I beg and take a step toward him, and he makes a threatening move closer to the edge of the building.

"Hey, man, dwadillypod, right?" says Corey. "That's what you always say to us when we get down in the dumps."

"Yeah, to hell with, dwadillypod! I've had it with all of this crap. I can't stand it," says Bob, beginning to cry.

"Come down and we can talk . . . come up with a plan. Like beat the hell out of your brother. The three of us can take him. We'll tell him if he ever lays a hand on you again, he'll have the Gargoyle's to deal with," offers Corey.

"Yeah, we're Gargoyle's, and we can fly," says Bob doing a full circle on the ledge and almost losing his balance.

"Don't move!" I shout, and Bob's weeping is replaced by weird laughter.

"Wouldn't it be funny if I jumped and landed on my lousy brother's head? I think he's down there, the scuzzball. Splat! Flatten him out like a pancake. Yeah, look, I think I see him," says Bob pointing down toward the street, but when we move toward the ledge he again orders us to stop.

"Maybe I'll just stay airborne a while. You know, fly around the city. I could crap on him like a seagull, only with bigger turds," says Bob laughing wildly at the idea.

He then looks at us hard and asks something that really seems creepy considering where we are. "Hey, you guys smell some fudge baking? Some dwadilly-fucking-fudge? I do. I mean I can really smell it."

Suddenly two adults emerge from the stairwell, and Bob warns them to stay where they are. One is a uniformed policeman and the other is dressed in a suit and tie. We're ordered off the roof, and the man in the suit barks for Bob to get down from the ledge. To our amazement, Bob does as he's ordered, and the officer and man grab him by his arms.

"You stupid little bastards. What is this some kind of game of dare?" asks the man in the suit, who I deduce is a plain clothes cop—a detective.

We try to explain the situation, but do not get far before we are directed down the stairs to a waiting police car.

"We'll talk about this back at the police station," says the detective, and we're taken away.

"What are your names?" asks the uniformed cop and we tell him.

When it is Bob's turn, he blurts out "Dwadillypod" and repeats the goofy word all the way to the police station, even though both the cops have told him to shut his trap.

Bailed Out

It is well after midnight before Corey and I are released from police custody. The manager of the Biltmore is not pressing trespassing charges, but we are given a stern warning never to return to the hotel. We learn that Bob is taken to a hospital for mental observation. It happens to be the same place that his mom is being kept, so he makes a crack about having a family reunion as they escort him from the police station. Meanwhile his brother is being sought for beating him up but seems to have disappeared.

Corey's mom gets to the police station first and quickly whisks him away without so much as a hello. About a half hour later my dad fetches me. Needless to say he's not happy about what has happened and all the way home he lectures me about my criminal behavior, as he calls it, and the bad choices I have made in the selection of my friends.

"That kid, Bob, is a nut case like his whole family. His mom is a psycho and his brother is a real thug. Always drunk and in trouble."

When I attempt to defend Bob, my father tells me to keep my mouth closed and just listen.

"That little darky is another doozey. And I don't care if he is a dwarf. He's got trouble written all over him. You hang out with him and you're going down the same road. Those blackies are mostly hoodlums, so you associate with him and that's what you are."

"He wasn't even with us!" I protest, adding "Besides his mom is real nice."

"Look, you're a decent boy, and I don't want to see you with those kids. They're trouble," replies my dad his voice softening.

"What about Corey?" I protest.

"He's the best of the lot. Look, just stay away from all of them and find some new friends. Decent ones," he suddenly barks. "You can spend a little more time with your family for a change, too. You don't seem to care about the fact that your mom's been very sick. All you and your sister do is make a mess of the house and expect your mom to clean up after you. Well that's going to stop right now, buster."

I'm relieved that my mother and sister are in bed when we get home, so there is no further discussion of the matter. However, I expect a full-blown inquisition tomorrow at the breakfast table. My attic chamber is freezing as usual, and I quickly get under the covers without even removing my clothes. It's the coldest area in the house during the winter, because its radiator is always the last one to be reached by the heat and then it clangs and groans like something being tortured.

Drifting off to sleep I wonder if Bob will be given electroshock treatment like his mom and if he'll be permanently crazy like her. My last conscious thoughts are about Mr. Brennan smothering his sick wife and dead little Sara staring at me on the Flo from the tall marsh grass on Prudence Island. Maybe Flo and Sara know one another in the place where dead people inhabit. Why do some spirits continue to have a presence on earth while others never appear again, I wonder, as my lids grow heavy and finally close down on my tired eyes?

Shrinking Circle

On a Friday, Corey says goodbye.

"We're going for a visit down under for a couple weeks," he says as if he is just going on a day trip to Cape Cod.

I feel glum about his trip to a place that, I'm sure, will become his new home. I remember that he'd always seemed to be somewhere else. I wonder if this is where. Even Henry, who never was all that chummy with Corey, seems sad at the prospect of his leaving, but I wonder if it's just an act.

There are no long farewells on Saturday because he's departing for Australia at sunrise, flying out of Boston, he says, and I'm excited just hearing him talk about being on an airplane for almost two days, since I have never been on one at all. So just like that the ranks of the Gargoyles is reduced to two for the time being, and maybe even permanently, not that Henry cares because he is not an official member of the ledge walkers club even though he accompanies us to rooftops on occasion. It appears the Gargoyles could become extinct, especially since Bob is now living in Cranston with his new court appointed guardians and rarely makes it up to Providence. When he does, the last thing he wants to do is walk on roof top ledges, although he still wants to get a bum to buy him wine. He says his foster parents are okay but doesn't elaborate beyond that.

Since Henry is not welcome at my house and Corey is no longer around, the days are draggy and lonely. In the absence of my cohorts, I make more frequent visits to Mary Kay's house. She's making real progress as the strength is returning to her legs, and we sometimes take pretty long walks, once reaching within a couple blocks of school. Icy sidewalks curtail our activities somewhat, so we play cards and Monopoly at Mary Kay's kitchen table while her mother makes brownies and cookies for us.

"Has Mr. Brennan done any more about the Clayburgh's boat?" she asks, and I inform her that he has taken the Flo out of the water for the winter but intends on collecting more evidence when the weather warms up.

"I want to go with you when you go looking. By then, I'll be able to help," says Mary Kay in a whisper, but she's overheard by her mom.

"Honey, it would be very dangerous to be on a boat in your condition. What if you fell overboard? You wouldn't be able to swim," she says, a look of grave concern covering her face.

"I'd rescue her," I say, secretly doubting that I could, and Mrs. Walton pats my shoulder and acknowledges my courage.

"I know you'd try, David, but it would be very hard to help her with those braces on. It's better to avoid situations like that."

"But mom," protests Mary Kay, "I'd be wearing a life preserver, and Mr. Brennan's boat would never sink. It's all fixed up like new. I'm going."

"We'll talk about this another time, sweetie. Besides, the police are probably going to take over the search for the Clayburgh's boat. It's really their business, and civilians shouldn't be interfering in their work."

When Mrs. Walton leaves the kitchen, Mary Kay announces that she plans to go with us when we set sail for Prudence Island in the spring.

"Not sure I'm going," I confess. "I think Mr. Brennan is a little loony-tunes, and I don't know if it's safe to be out on his boat."

"Why?" asks Mary Kay.

"Oh, nothing really. He's just a little weird. That's all. Besides I'm kind of tired with the whole Clayburgh thing."

"Have you been seeing Sara anymore?' inquires Mary Kay.

"Naw," I reply, lying between my teeth. "I just think they're gone and the whole thing should be forgotten."

"But it's such a mystery, and you know the house is haunted. You say you hear things coming from it at night. Maybe they're trying to tell you something. Maybe they want you to find their boat so their spirits can be released and they can go to heaven."

"It's nothing like that," I protest.

"What about the letter? Bet Mr. Clayburgh found out his wife had a boyfriend and did something awful."

"Mr. Brennan took the letter to the police. He made up a story about finding it stuck in the hedges next to the Polio House so they wouldn't figure he was trespassing. They said the letter doesn't mean anything, doesn't prove a thing. It could be from anybody. I bet they think Mr. Brennan's just an old kook," I say trying to debunk the theory and steer the conversation in another direction.

"Well, you can't just turn your back on it. It's so awful what happened to the poor Clayburghs. A terrible tragedy, and they probably won't rest until it's all figured out. I think Sara is trying to tell you something."

"Forget about it!" I snap. "It's stupid to think there are ghosts anyway."

Mary Kay is surprised by my sudden anger and looks hurt and that immediately makes me feel crummy.

"I didn't mean you're stupid. I just don't think there are ghosts. That's all."

"But you said you saw Sara?" she says, her voice barely audible.

"I know, but I think I was just seeing things, so I'm trying to forget about it, okay?"

"Okay," says Mary Kay, clearing the Monopoly board even though the game is not over. "Just pretend you didn't see what you know you saw, Ketch."

Down to One

I take up with Henry again, who's just as pleased as I am that we have one another to hang out with. Of course, this requires keeping our friendship a secret from my family, especially my father. Making new buddies doesn't seem in the cards for us, particularly since neither one of us is really trying all that much.

After school we spend time in the asylum, but it's not the same without Bob and Corey, and Henry is the first to admit that.

"Don't know what the big deal was bein' in this ole cold buildin' anyhow," he says, as we fiddle unenthusiastically with the controls of the broken electroshock machine. "My fingers are so cold I can't feel the knobs," he complains. "The best thing to do is make us a fire with some of the wood pieces around here so we don't get frostbite."

"No fires," I say.

"Don't worry," he replies. "You got to make it so it don't catch onto nothing. Put it right there in the middle of the room. It can't catch onto nothing there.

'Sides we're only gonna make a little one just to warm us up some," he says.

"I'll leave," I threaten, and Henry starts to go.

"Forget this place," he says. "Shiiitt!"

We climb through the boarded exit—Henry, then me—and out onto the chilly street.

"We got to find some place else to hang out and it better have heat 'cause I ain't gonna' freeze my butt off," says Henry rubbing his thick hind end in an attempt to warm it.

The problem of where to spend time that offers us shelter from the winter elements is not an easy one to solve. Henry thinks we should hang out at his house even if my house is off limits to him, but I feel funny about that because it doesn't seem fair.

"You're ashamed to be goin' to a colored's house, I think. That's why you ain't been there so long," says Henry.

"It has nothing to do with that," I protest, but Henry doesn't buy it.

"Sure, Ketch. You just love hangin' out with this nigger who ain't got normal size."

"Hey, don't say that! You're my best friend now, and if you were green and ten feet tall it wouldn't matter," I reply defensively.

"Really?" asks Henry his hard expression softening. "Well, you're my best friend, too, even though you're the ugliest commie I ever set eyes on."

With no place in particular to go, we wander the snowy city streets. An hour into our aimless excursion, we catch sight of the hot rod punks and hide in a doorway until they are safely out of sight.

"Damn!" complains Henry, "Can't even go nowhere without gettin' to someplace crappy. I'm just goin' home."

I'm left standing alone in the grimy doorway as he heads off in the direction of his house. Right there and then I decide to make some new pals. Maybe my dad's right. It doesn't look right if my only friends are a colored midget, a cripple, and a little girl ghost. Maybe the Boil Man at the bus station is looking for a friend, I muse, as I drift back toward my neighborhood feeling that my prospects have hit a new low.

Another Little Friend

On the day Corey is due back from Australia there's a snowstorm, what my father calls a Nor'easter. Overnight a half-foot of snow falls and school is canceled. By late morning it's still coming down, and I meet up with Henry at the park to go sledding. We use large pieces of cardboard to fly down the small hill because neither one of us has a good sled. Mine is old and hard to drag any distance, and Henry's sled has a broken runner, which gets stuck in the snow and slows its speed. Cardboard works just fine, but there's no way to steer and nothing to really hold onto, so half the time you fall off before you get to the bottom of the hill. In the summer we used to roll down the hill inside cardboard boxes, but that ended when I fractured my arm.

At the park we run into a kid named Emil Broder, who we met the week before when he cleaned us out of baseball cards. When he won Henry's favorite Ted Williams card, I thought for sure a fight would start, but instead Henry acted like it was no big deal. He likes Emil because he's very short. Not a midget but close to it. In fact, he's only slightly taller than Henry. Emil is a year younger than us, which I figure accounts for his size. He was skipped a grade because he's very smart, but the other kids pick on him almost as much as they pick on Henry. I get off a little easier because my height is average, although I'm too skinny so I get teased plenty for that.

"Stand sideways and stick out your tongue and you look like a dick pokin' out of a fly," jokes Henry to my great dissatisfaction because I hate comments about being so bony.

Emil may be short, but his weight is normal, unlike Henry whose body is stubby and broad. As it turns out Emil lives only a couple of blocks away from my house where he's lived for just a couple of months. His family moved down from Worcester so his father could take a better paying job as a foreman at Emblem and Badge.

"He makes trophies," he tells us, and promises to get us one with Gargoyles engraved on it.

I come up with a contest that will determine whose the best ledge walker of us all.

"You're the only one now, so that ain't much of a contest," observes Henry, but Emil says he wants to give Gargoyling a try.

"Corey comes home today, and Bob will come up, too," I say in rebuttal.

"They're crazy, Emil. Why you wanna go gettin' yourself splattered like them?" asks Henry shaking his big head in disapproval.

"I like to climb tall things, too," responds Emil, and Henry adds that he's just acting like all the other crazy white boys.

"Least my mama gave me some sense. How come yours didn't do that, too? Shhiiit," he says flopping his chunky torso onto his cardboard sled and shooting down the snowy embankment.

"Really, I want to join the Gargloyals," says Emil, and I correct his pronunciation of our soon to be revived club.

"When some of the snow melts from the roofs, we'll have our contest and you can join us," I tell our new member, who, smiling broadly, promises to have the trophy ready by then.

Henry stands at the bottom of the hill waving for us to join him. I hit the cardboard and push off with my feet, but Emil decides to walk down the hill saying he doesn't like sliding so fast. This makes me wonder if he'll really have the courage to walk the ledges of tall buildings.

On my descent to the bottom, I look back at Emil as he begins to trail me on foot. The further down I get, the smaller he looks, and for one split second he becomes somebody else. In his place at the top of the hill is dead Sara, and I fall off the cardboard and go toppling to where Henry is waiting.

"You better stick to climbin' them buildings, 'cause you sure ain't no sledder," says Henry helping me to my feet.

When I look back up the hill, Emil is trudging down and waving at us. There is no sign of Sara, and I figure that snow in bright sunlight can probably cause mirages like on a burning desert.

The Aussie

Two days later when most of the snow has melted because the temperature has risen to nearly 50 degrees, Corey drops by. Australia is really great he says, and he hopes he gets to move there.

"It's much prettier than here, and it's warmer. You should see the kangaroos. They know how to box. Can kick your ass, too. Here, I got you this. It's a boomerang. You throw it and it comes back to you."

He actually seems to have grown in the two weeks he's been away, and when I make that observation, he says it's the new boots he's wearing.

"They got real big heels, and they're made from a crocodile," he remarks tugging up his pant leg so I can get a full view. "You can get belts and other stuff made from them, too. My mom got a crocodile purse."

The idea of killing animals, even ugly crocodiles, to make things out of them disturbs me, and when I say so, Corey says they attack and eat people. Still the idea of making stuff out of their skin strikes me as pretty mean, and when I make that observation, he remarks that if you don't get them they'll make a dinner out of you, which is pretty mean, too.

"If you ever saw one of them, you'd change your mind real fast. They're real ugly, and they got hundreds of fangs. They can gobble you up in two gulps."

He saw some at a crock farm, as he calls it, outside of Sydney that also had giant snakes. As much as I like animals, I have no interest in reptiles. Again, I proclaim that creatures like that are not going to be a part of my veterinarian practice, if that's what I become.

Despite the fact that my father ordered me to stay away from Corey after we all got caught on the roof of the Biltmore, he greets him with mild enthusiasm.

"David says you been away. Out there in Australia, right?

"Just got back, Mr. Ketchum. We might move there permanently," responds Corey, who I calculate is now about an inch taller than my dad.

"Don't think I'd care for that place," replies my father ending the conversation by opening his paper so he's hidden behind it.

After a few moments of awkward silence we leave the house and head to the asylum to meet up with Emil and Henry. On the way Corey continues to talk about how great Australia is compared to dumpy old Providence.

"Sydney has taller buildings," he claims and says he plans to start a new chapter of the Gargoyles when he moves there. "Kids are really friendly there, too, so I bet I can get a lot to join the club."

His enthusiasm for what may become his new home fills me with envy, because I know I'll probably never get to move to a new place, at least not until I'm grown up.

Then I'll go someplace better than Providence and start a hospital for dogs like Topper that have problems with gas and other stuff.

"G'day, mate," says Corey to Henry when we reach the asylum.

"You're talkin' like somethin's stuck under your tongue. Like a big ole turd, maybe," responds Henry, and I quickly introduce Emil to prevent tensions from growing.

Abandoning his Aussie accent, Corey says he's glad to meet him. Next to Corey, Emil and Henry look like third graders.

"You're only in ninth grade?" asks Emil, and Henry jokes that Corey stayed back four times because he couldn't talk like normal people.

"Maybe you won't be talking right if I shove this in your kisser," responds Corey clenching his fist in mock anger.

Inside the asylum we introduce Emil to the shock room and Henry tells him that it was used to shoot electricity up the wazoos of crazy people.

"They take this rod and shove it up here," he says sticking his hand into Emil's backside and causing him to jump away. "Hey, you got a pretty nice butt. Maybe I give you my cukey," he jokes, but Emil reacts angrily shoving Henry's hand away from him.

"Don't worry, boy. I ain't no homo like them guys," he says pointing to Corey and me, and we both tell him to clamp it.

We give Emil a tour of the rest of the asylum ending up at the dining room entrance. When we approach it Emil asks what the smell is. The aroma brings me goose bumps and it stops us in our tracks.

"Smells like fudge baking," observes Corey, and this adds more bumps to the ones I already have.

We slowly open the door to the room, and when we do the smell becomes stronger.

"Someone must be cooking," remarks Emil oblivious to the significance of what we're experiencing because we haven't told him this part of the asylum's creepy history. "Let's go check it out," he suggests, and we stop him and give him a quick account of the poisoned fudge that killed two people.

Emil looks at us skeptically but follows along closely as we quickly make our way out of the building. We can still detect the smell once out on the sidewalk.

"Maybe it's coming from that chimney across the street," says Emil pointing to a thick plume of dark smoke swirling in the air above a building with an auto body shop.

For Emil's benefit we elaborate on the story about how the asylum's crazy inmates could smell fudge baking even when the chocolate factory no longer existed.

"It was the curse of that guy who put arsenic in the fudge," adds Henry as we look at the former chocolate factory and nut house. "His ghost's still in there brewing up some more them deadly brownies."

"There isn't anybody in there," says Corey, attempting to debunk the idea but not doing so very convincingly. "Just our imaginations going kookie again, like you and that Sara girl, Ketch. Our brains are just playing tricks on us."

"But we all smelled the fudge," I protest, and Corey just shrugs while Henry and Emil shake their heads in agreement.

"Bet it was just because we had that stupid fudge story in our heads already," says Corey, and I remind him that Emil thought he smelled the fudge, too, even though he had not actually said that.

"So what're you gonna' say now, crocodile man?" says Henry, and Corey replies we're all getting loopy from spending so much time in the dark old building and pointing up at the dense chimney smoke now hanging on it.

"Ghosts are bad enough, but when they're fudge sniffing crazy ones, you better watch your butt for sure," says Henry, his expression stone serious.

We leave the scene and the conversation turns to the upcoming ledge-walking tournament. Emil says he'll have the trophy in a couple days, so plans are set for the contest to determine who is the champion building walker of the world. Since the Biltmore is now off limits, we're going to attempt to access the roof of the Union Trust Company, a twelve story building down on Dorrance Street.

"They got a great ledge there. It's held up by these cement columns so it's like walking on a fence that's on top of a skyscraper," I report having scouted out the building.

"Twelve stories ain't no skyscraper, but I suppose you die just as fast if you fall off it," is Henry's parting remark as we leave one another's company for our own houses.

And the Champion Is

Bob has come up from Cranston to observe the contest. He has no plans to compete, but there is a lack of conviction in his voice, and we figure he'll join in once things get going. Getting to the top of the building poses no great challenge to us. It's just a matter of reaching up high enough to catch the bottom of the fire escape in the back of the building. We accomplish this by getting Emil on to Corey's shoulders so he can make the grab with the handle of an old umbrella we bring along. In a couple minutes the four of us are admiring the view of the city from the roof.

There is a narrow transom in the middle of the roof, and Corey sprawls across it's dark opening like he is lying in a hammock. He cradles the trophy Emil has supplied on his stomach, occasionally standing it upright and balancing it.

"Wake me when you guys are done, so I can win this thing and go home," he jokes acting like the whole thing is just a big bore.

Emil climbs onto the building's ledge immediately and takes a few quick steps. I warn him about going too fast and to avoid looking at the ground below because he may get vertigate.

"Vertigo," says Corey correcting me.

"What's that?' asks Emil, and Corey explains that some people get dizzy when they're up high.

"Not me. I'm fine," replies Emil moving along the ledge.

Bob lingers next to the transom where Corey continues to straddle himself. He says he is content just to watch us climb around.

"Maybe I'll do some ledge walking the next time," he remarks unconvincingly.

"You've gone soft since you moved," observes Corey.

"Nah, just don't care about doing it," says Bob with a distant look in his eyes. "Don't really care about nothing a lot of the time and that kind of pisses off my foster parents. They don't say much but I can tell they're not happy when I get quiet and stay in my room. Just don't feel like doing things, like play stupid board games with their other foster kids. Maybe I'm like that Rebel Without A Cause kid in the movie."

"No, you're more like the Soap without a Rope kid" jokes Corey, who starts talking about Australia again, and we listen as he tells us about going to a huge red rock in the center of the country where short dark people called aboriginals still run around naked.

"Some had pants on, but mostly they were in their birthday suites with cloths over their privates. We saw some in Sydney, too, but they had regular clothes on."

Bob asks if they are like colored people, and Corey says they looked more like a combination of Indians and Africans and maybe a little bit like cavemen, adding that some had blond hair.

"That's weird," observes Bob his face crinkled like he is trying to imagine what they would look like. "I don't know if I'd like to live there or not."

"Thought you wanted to move there? Boy, you don't know what the heck you want. Next thing you'll be doing is serving mass with Father Carter," says Corey.

"No way I'm going to be an alter boy for that fruity priest," replies Bob, and we all laugh.

An hour or so later we're set to go when we notice Emil climbing across the transom.

"Hey, I wouldn't try that!" shouts Corey. "You're too small to reach the sides."

"I'm fine," responds Emil trying to drape himself over the opening, but his body is not long enough to make contact with the transom's ends.

Corey reaches Emil just as he starts to lose his grip, and in one swift grab, he snags him as he's about to fall down the dark shaft.

"Holy dwadillypod!" exclaims Bob shaking his head.

"Yeah, dwadillypod," I repeat breathlessly as Corey places Emil safely away from the hole that nearly gobbled him.

"You saved my life," gasps Emil, climbing to his feet and straightening his clothes. "Thanks. I mean . . . really, thanks!"

"Don't mention it. All in a day's work," replies Corey with a smug expression that doesn't completely hide his rattled nerves. "Just don't do it again. I can only save one life a day."

With that close call we climb down from the rooftop, and as soon as we reach the ground, we split up and head to our own houses. When someone almost dies, it leaves you kind of speechless.

White and Black

It has snowed overnight again. Not a lot, but at least a couple inches, and it always makes the Polio House look even more eerie, especially with the icicles that have form on its gutters. They hang down like vampire fangs, and when I steal a look at the place, I'm thankful there's no sign of little Sara. It's been a long time since I've sensed her presence, and I'm beginning to wonder if she's just given up on haunting me, or whether my imagination isn't working overtime like everyone says it does. If I'm lucky she has taken to haunting some other person.

It's Saturday and I have plans to meet up with Corey and Henry to go to the asylum to hang out. Corey shows up shortly after I've eaten a bowl of cheerios and a piece of cinnamon toast. We're supposed to meet Henry at the corner, because he doesn't want to encounter my father, who doesn't want to see him either. My mom and sister are still in bed, but my dad is up and trying to fix a leaky pipe under the kitchen sink. He's no expert at such things, he admits, but he does claim to be handier than most men around the house.

"It may not be very pretty when I'm done, but it usually works," he has boasted on more than one occasion after making a repair.

Today he says nothing while he's clunking around under the drippy sink, and when I lead Corey into the kitchen, he just waves in his direction with his wrench.

I gulp down the remains of my orange juice, put on my coat and hat, and we head out to meet up with Henry, who Corey bets won't be on time.

"He's never there when he says he will be," Corey complains, "so there's no need to rush. It's just 8 o'clock on the dot, and he won't be there until quarter after, I bet."

Thinking he's probably right, I flop down on the front room couch, and Corey follows suit.

"So what kind of schools do they have in Australia?" I ask, and Corey replies that they're much nicer than the ones here.

"How so?" I inquire, and he replies that they aren't all gloomy and old looking and have better fields and sports stadiums.

"They have nice chairs and not cold cement steps to sit on, so people there don't get piles like they do here from watching games."

After listing a whole bunch more reasons why going to school in Australia is better than going to school in South Providence, Corey says we can go meet Henry now that it's quarter after the hour.

"He's usually fifteen minutes late, so he should be there now."

As we move down the steps of my house, we can see Henry's small form at the corner and he sees us too. He throws his hands in the air, which is what he does a lot when he is po'd. He lets loose his fury when we reach him.

"I been waitin' here for 15 minutes, while you jokers be nice and warm. I been freezin' my agates off. Maybe I'm not good enough to come to your house, Ketch, but I'm better than let freeze out here."

We apologize, remarking that he's usually late, but he's having none of it and keeps shooting angry words at us. Finally, Corey tells him to zip it or he's going back home, and that cools things down as we continue in the direction of the asylum.

The snow is nearly ankle deep and every so often the wind whips up the dry crystals creating a brief blizzard that decreases visibility to almost nothing. Just as quickly everything settles down and the street ahead is perfectly clear. This happens several times before we reach our destination and we enjoy the dramatic effect.

"They don't get snowy days like this down under," remarks Corey in the middle of one of the mini storms.

After a silence Henry pipes up with a question intended to further irk Corey. "Why they call it 'down under? 'Cause it's like a crotch, all sweaty and stinky?"

"No," replies Corey, ignoring Henry's sarcasm but getting in a dig of his own, "because it's below the equator. Anyone with brains knows that."

"Anybody with brains don't go to a place that's under everything," quips Henry, and Corey just shakes his head in disgust.

We head around to the side of the asylum to the drain pipe leading to the window we use to gain entrance and immediately realize that something is different about it. It has new boards across it and is firmly secured. When we check out other windows on the street level, we discover they, too, have brand new boards across them and are nailed down. Corey gives a hard yank to the boards, but they don't budge even for him. We try several other windows within our reach, but the place is closed tighter than Fort Knox, according to Henry.

"That ends goin' in that creepy place," he remarks with a faint smile of satisfaction. "Now we got to find someplace else to hang out, and I ain't hangin' out on top of no building in this freezin' weather either."

Corey says he's not in the mood to go looking for someplace else to hang out and announces he's going home, adding that his feet are cold and wet from the snow anyway because he forgot to wear his crocodile boots.

"You got any money for a soda?" inquires Henry as we head back from the asylum.

I haven't but suggest I go ask my mother for some. Henry thinks that's a good idea, but warns me against making him wait outside too long.

"I'm about froze solid already," he complains, and then suggests we slip into the Polio House after we get soda and make a fire to warm us up.

The idea strikes me as totally nuts, and I tell him so, which launches him into more complaints about not being allowed into my house to get warm.

"Your daddy's one of them damn bigots. My uncle Willie says bigots hanged poor black folks and burned their houses in the south when he was a boy. Maybe I'll burn some white folk's house down," growls Henry removing a box of wooden matches from his coat pocket and displaying them to give his threat credence.

"What if you killed somebody?" I ask him, not imagining he could do that.

"Don't want to hurt nobody. Just take away from them what they took from poor colored people" he responds returning the matches to his pocket.

Boxed In

My mom says I can have money for sodas, but to get it I have to run an errand for her. She needs another one of her brown boxes. I protest knowing that Henry is going to make a big deal out of it, but my mom insists I go to the store for her no matter what excuses I make up. I reluctantly take the money for what she calls her sanitary napkins and she adds some change for me to get what I want.

"Linda's not here, or I'd have her go for me," she says, seeing my pained expression. "Now don't be so silly about this. It's a perfectly normal thing."

"Then how come they wrap them up in a brown box with no names on it?" I reply, and my mom says to keep silly boys like me from being embarrassed. "It doesn't help," I protest, "because everybody knows what they are."

Exasperated, she practically pushes me out the front door along with Topper saying he needs to be walked before he has an accident. Henry sees me and waves, and as we walk toward one another, I try to figure out how to keep my humiliating mission from him but realize there's no way I can so decide to just tell him and face the music.

"I got to get my mom some of them Kotex things," I admit, bracing myself for what is certain to follow.

To my surprise and relief, like Corey, Henry acts like it's no big thing admitting his mom makes him go to the store for them, too, which he doesn't like anymore than me.

"It's women business, but I sure wish they'd get 'em themselves. It don't really bother me no more. I figure it can't be too much fun for them to go through that menstring stuff every month. Least we don't do all that bleedin'. So goin' to the store ain't so bad is what I think."

I'm impressed by Henry's mature attitude and figure I'll try not to let it bother me anymore, concluding that my mom has to deal with the bleeding plus her polio so I should be better about it for her sake.

"Ain't no fun being no women, cause they got to make babies, and I don't see how they do that. Sure must hurt having some big ole kid come out that little place between their legs. You imagine that? It hurts for me to pass a hard turd, and it's only this big compared to this big," says Henry demonstrating the difference in the size of a turd versus a newborn baby.

We purchase my mom's brown box and a couple sodas and stop to drink them in the field next to the store. Henry says his feet feel frozen, so he's going home and soak them in some hot water to keep from getting frostbite.

"I think they already might be," he says as we leave the field, and just as we do, the car with the punks pulls up next to us from out of nowhere, and I know we're in for trouble.

"Ignore them, I say to Henry. "Just keep walking. You can come in my house until they leave."

The car stops and one of the greasers climbs out and blocks our path.

"Where you little douche bags going?" he asks, placing his hands against our chests.

"None your business," blurts out Henry, whose fists are clenched.

"Hey, Mark, we got a wise little coon here. We must be in the niggerhood," he shouts to the other teen in the car, who gets out and joins his friend.

They're both at least a foot taller than me and twice that much taller than Henry.

"We're going," I say, trying to push pass them, but I'm stopped in my tracks.

"Where'd you get that big black ugly head, coon boy?" spouts the first boy who's sporting a duck's ass haircut glistening with goop and a black leather jacket, and Henry's eyes have narrowed to two menacing slits.

"Never saw a nigger midget," chimes in the second boy, and with that Henry throws a hard punch to his crotch area causing him to topple to the ground.

This earns him a swift crack in the eye from the first boy, which causes Topper to growl and bark at the punk. When he attempts to kick Topper, everything that's been building in me lets loose and I blast Henry's attacker in the kisser as hard as I can with my mom's Kotex box, causing him to fall backwards over his moaning friend. We then make a run for it and in seconds reach my house. Instead of following me inside though Henry continues running as fast as his small legs can carry him in the direction of his own house, his hand pressed against his wounded face.

Wanderings

Two days have passed since I've seen Henry, and I wonder how he is. He's not in school the Monday following the fight with the punks, and I'm thinking he was tracked down by those guys and really beat up bad. I'm frightened they may track me down, too, and do the same. Because of this I keep a watch out in all directions when I'm outside. For a split second on my way home after school, I think I spot the greaser's jalopy and dodge behind a tree. I'm relieved when it only turns out to be a car that looks like theirs.

After supper I head over to Mary Kay's for a visit. She has asked me to bring Topper, because she loves his big furry body and hasn't got a dog of her own anymore. Her dog, named Spuds, died of old age just after she got polio and her parents haven't wanted to replace him until Mary Kay recovers more. When I think about it, bringing Topper with me is a good idea, because I know he'd protect me if the jerks in the car show up.

Mrs. Walton answers the door. She's gussied up for her visit to school where she's attending a parent/teacher's meeting to discuss Mary Kay returning in the fall.

"Hello, David. Mary Kay is watching TV in the living room. I'm glad you brought Topper. Mary Kay loves dogs. We'll be getting a new one soon."

Topper runs over to Mary Kay, who is propped up with several pillows on the couch. She squeals when Topper leaps up next to her, and I shout for him to get down, but Mrs. Walton just laughs and says he's fine, delighted with her daughter's reaction.

"Okay, you kids have fun watching TV. I'll be back in about an hour," says Mrs. Walter, putting on her coat and exiting.

Mary Kay tells me to turn off the TV so that she can play me her newest and favorite song by Julius LaRosa, called "Any Where I Wander." I put the record on the turntable and sit on the couch next to her as Topper flops on the rug nearby.

"Don't you like it?" she asks, humming along. "It makes me feel happy."

I figure the idea of wandering and roaming around, as the lyrics say, is what most appeals to her about the song.

"Daddy is coming home in a couple weeks," announces Mary Kay, the sparkle in her eyes is brighter than I have ever seen it. "He's been at sea for almost nine months. He'll be excited to see me walking so well. When he left I could hardly take two steps. Now I can walk at least twenty before taking a rest. I know I'll be ready for school when it starts."

When the song ends, she asks me to put it on one more time, and after it plays, we go back to watching TV. With her legs covered by a blanket, no one could tell that she's so crippled, and I feel that I could marry her, but when I catch sight of her crutches resting against the end table, I have doubts again. Maybe she'll grow out of them like kids do their clothes, yet with bent limbs like she has I kind of doubt it.

We're watching "Ozzie and Harriet" when Mary Kay asks if I want to kiss. Sure, I say surprised, and we press our lips together briefly and then again for a longer time. As our mouths are locked, I move to open her blouse, but then Topper lets out a blast of gas and we can't stop laughing. Thankfully, it also takes the air out of my cukey that had started to swell the longer I had contact with Mary Kay. Eventually, we shift our attention back to the TV screen, as Ricky is lectured by his dad, Mr. Nelson, for doing something silly.

The Offer

After a week Henry returns to school. Midway through the week, I had gone to Henry's house and rang the doorbell, but no one answered, and I wondered if he and his mother moved back south. Henry says he just didn't want to come back to school with a big lump on his face. There's still a welt next to his eye, but unless you're looking closely you wouldn't notice it because his dark skin seems to absorb it.

"My mama was gonna put me in the Catholic school to get me away from this place, but I didn't want to go there and wear no dumb uniform, so she let me come back. Ain't gonna play no hooky no more cause I wanna get my diploma and make somethin' of myself. Mama says that's the only way to get away from white trash punks who hate coloreds."

Henry says I better stay away from his house for a while because his mama and uncles are mad at all white boys right now for what happened to him.

"I told her you helped me fight those jackasses, but she's so mad at everyone white that she told me to stay with my own kind. Even though I told her they ain't no colored kids I like the way I like you, it don't matter while she's so angry. I gotta keep my distance is what she says."

For the rest of the day Henry steers clear of me and practically everybody, except for a Chinese kid, who never really talks to anyone.

A surprise awaits me as I return home from school. Sitting in the living room with my mom is Father Carter, and I think he is there to report my dirty confession.

"David, look who's here," says my mom in a way that makes me think Father Carter hasn't yet revealed my crime.

In an overly friendly manner that makes me really suspicious about what is to come, the priest greets me with a broad smile and extended hand, which I shake with a growing sense of panic.

"Good to see you, young man," he remarks, and I wonder how that can be since I haven't been back to confession since the joke we pulled on him. "He's a fine lad, one we like to have help us serve mass. What do you think, David? Would you like to be an altar boy?"

I'm left speechless and begin to think he's getting even by playing a joke on me, but then I can tell from my mom's expression that it's something he's already discussed with her.

"Well, David, would you like to be Father Carter's altar boy?" asks my mom staring at me as I say nothing. After an awkward silence, she says, "Maybe he'd like to think about it, Father. Would that be okay?"

"Certainly. It is a big commitment and we don't want to force anybody into assisting with the holy Eucharist unless they really want to. Why don't you come by the rectory, David, and tell me your decision when you make up your mind, but don't wait too long. There are other boys who would like the chance to serve God."

I manage a nod, and Father Carter departs after thanking my mom for the tea she has given him. When he's out of the house my mom says I wasn't very grateful to Father Carter for the honor he wants to bestow on me.

"Sorry," I reply, and my mom says that while she'd love me to become an altar boy it's my decision and I should think seriously about it.

"I will," I promise and head up to my room.

For a moment I'm tempted to tell her why I don't want to be Father Carter's altar boy, but then I decide against it thinking it would probably lead to telling her about the dirty story I told him in confession and about skipping confession for weeks when she thought I was going. Although my parents seldom attend church, they take my following the church's rules seriously.

When my sister hears of Father Carter's offer to make me an altar boy she teases me saying that the church's ceiling will collapse if I step foot on the altar. Even though her reaction is one more thing that makes me mad at her, I confide about my concerns and experience with the priest. At first, she claims I'm just making it up but then she begins to believe what I'm telling her.

"You should tell mom," she suggests, but I say it would just upset her and that wouldn't be good because she's still getting over her polio.

"Maybe you could tell dad then," she counters, and I protest citing his bad mood lately.

"Yeah, he's been grumpy. That's for sure," she replies.

We decide to hold off on any action at this time until we can come up with a better plan. In the meantime, Linda suggests I just tell my parents I don't want to be an altar boy without explaining why.

"Just say you don't like wearing those frilly gowns they make you put on," she jokes, and I think that's not such a bad idea.

Skin Deep

I can't get the Boil Man out of my mind so after school I head down to the Greyhound station to check him out again. It doesn't take long to spot him. He's unloading the luggage compartment below a bus onto a flatbed cart and his boils are every bit as revolting to me as they were when I saw him with Corey and Bob. How does it happen that a person becomes covered by millions of pea size bumps, I wonder, and I follow the Boil Man with my eyes as he moves the loaded luggage cart to an area next to the Traveler's Aid station in the center of the bus depot. There he unloads the suitcases and boxes.

I'm not the only person intrigued by his gruesome appearance. Every time someone catches sight of him, their eyes widen and they quickly avert their stare so they don't embarrass the poor man if he sees them gawking. Apparently being stared at is nothing new to him, because when some young kids do, his eyes pass over them like they're not there.

Does someone that ghastly looking have a family, and do they suffer from the same terrible affliction, I ponder, along with a bunch of other questions? How could someone without a million mammoth pimples marry someone who looks like the Creature From the Black Lagoon? Does he live alone in some dark cave because no one will associate with him? What if you had a father or brother who looked like that? Would you still love them? What would your friends think if they knew your father was the Boil Man? Would you even have any friends if your dad was covered with ugly lumps? A hundred thoughts fill my head as I continue to watch the Boil Man work. Then I decide to find out more about him by waiting around until he gets off work and by following him to where he lives.

It's 5 o'clock when the Boil Man puts on his hooded overcoat and leaves the terminal. The wind is blowing hard, and it has become dark as I follow him up Weybosset to Broad Street. He is actually moving in the direction of my neighborhood, and I wonder how close he lives to me. Wouldn't it be funny, I think, if he lived on the same block, although it doesn't seem likely, since I have never seen him around there before and he's not someone you forget once you have.

The temperature seems to have dropped tons of degrees while I waited for the Boil Man to leave work, and as I follow at a safe distance behind him my whole body feels frozen, especially the toes of my feet and my fingers tips, even with my gloves on. But I am not to be deterred in my mission to find out more about this strange person. Staying a safe distance behind him I see him slip inside the same liquor store where we get our wine. By the time he comes out of the store I am shivering to death and worried that I'll get frostbite or even pneumonia.

It's only about a block later that he climbs the steps of what I gather is his house. Before he reaches the top of the stairs the door swings open and a small girl with outstretched arms greets the Boil Man. Emerging from the house behind the little girl is a woman with bright red hair, who also wraps her arms around him. From where I'm standing I determine that neither have lumps on their skin. In fact, both are really pretty. Arm and arm they enter the house looking like the happiest family in the world.

It's clear that the Boil Man is deeply loved despite the growths that have turned his body into something freakish. All I can think of is one of my mom's favorite sayings: never judge a book by its cover. As I haul my frigid body the rest of the way home, I'm happy that the Boil Man has a better existence than I imagined someone looking like him could possibly have. My mom is also fond of saying that it's what's inside that counts.

Brennan's Stories

The Flo is wrapped like a giant package in a blue tarp in Mr. Brennan's driveway. I'm dropping by his house to see if he has any more thoughts on the Polio House letters, because I've been thinking about going back in and grabbing another one. If I do, it would be in the daylight. The thought of going in there at night gives goose flesh. In fact, going in there in the light gives me them to, and I don't know if I have the courage to do it.

After knocking several times on Mr. Brennan's front door because his doorbell is broken, the door finally creeps open.

"Hey, Ketch, where you been, ole mate? Thought you and your friends forgot where I lived," says the bent and ashen-faced figure in front of me.

The first thing that comes to mind is that Mr. Brennan must have polio, but then it occurs to me that he's probably too old to get it.

"'Excuse the appearance. Been feeling under the weather for a while. Doc says I got some prostate problems. Old man's disease. Lots of pain in the lower back and legs and not getting any better, but it will pass like it always does. Come on in," says Mr. Brennan, and I follow him into his cluttered living room where in the very middle stands a one armed manikin covered in a loose fitting black negligee.

"Keeps me company until Mrs. Brennan gets back from her sister's in Florida," remarks Mr. Brennan who sees me staring at the strange object. "Wife's older sister's got multiple sclerosis and can't care much for herself these days, so Flo stays with her."

This statement catches me off guard considering his confession about suffocating his wife to end her pain.

"But, I thought . . ." I begin, and Mr. Brennan chimes in.

"You didn't think I really killed her, did you?" he asks chuckling. "I was just telling you boys a whopper. It's tradition to tell tall tales when you're out at sea. Old sailor's favorite pastime. Nothing else to do when you're out there floating around. So you swabs bought the story hook, line, and sinker, eh?"

"Well, yes, I stammer, and Mr. Brannan looks pleased.

"Damn, thought for sure you young fellas would see right through it. Hear that Flo?" he says looking at the manikin, "The old guy still has it. I used to tell her some real tall tales, too, just to get a rise out of her, but she got wise after a while and didn't pay much attention."

Frankly, I'm not sure what to believe, figuring that Mr. Brennan could just be saying that he made the whole thing up to keep us from telling the cops about it. On the other hand, Corey said he thought the old guy was a little loony and could be just imagining he did things when he really didn't. I'm beginning to think Mr. Brennan is ditzy, because who in their right mind would have an almost naked manikin in his front room?

"So what brings you by, Master Ketch?" asks Mr. Brennan easing into a chair covered with a tattered and soiled blanket.

I'm still distracted by the whole conversation, but I manage to pull my thoughts together to reveal my idea about grabbing more letters from the Polio House.

"Been thinking about them letters myself," says Mr. Brennan, squirming in his chair like he can't get comfortable. "Not sure they mean much. Maybe the other envelopes just have bills and stuff like that in them. Wouldn't bother really."

His sudden lack of interest in the letters disappoints me.

"But they may tell us about what happened to the Clayburghs," I protest, and he says he doubts that, adding that he thinks the whole thing is not as mysterious as we've been thinking it is.

"But what about the piece of their boat we found in the bay?" I ask, challenging his change of view.

"Could have just gotten loose from its mooring and drifted over to the island where it sunk," he answers, and then he says something that changes everything. "Don't think they drowned at all. In fact I think they're alive and well."

"What do you mean?" I respond thinking he really has lost all his marbles.

"Friend of mine who's a janitor down at the police station says he heard the Clayburghs are living out there in Tennessee with a cousin. So they likely ain't dead after all, except for that little girl of theirs who died of the polio."

"Are you sure?" I ask still trying to grasp this revelation.

"Well, I'm sure that's what old Hank told me. Beyond that, who knows? Makes sense though. Don't you think?"

"I guess, " I respond, not really sure what to believe anymore.

"Hey, young fella', don't be so glum. World's full of other mysteries needing to be solved. We'll take the Flo out again when the weather gets warm. Was reading about an old schooner that went down two hundred years ago near Conanicut Island that was filled with gold coins. Been doing some calculations, and I'm pretty sure where it might be located, so we'll get out there and claim it. Get rich. What do you think about them apples, Ketch?"

Corey's opinion about Mr. Brennan being crazy confirms my belief that he's a lot smarter than most kids his age.

More Discoveries

Henry is still avoiding me at school, preferring the company of his Chinese friend, who I gather from his sullen expression isn't all that pleased he's been adopted by him. I have a feeling Henry is going to come around soon though, because he kind of nodded at me in the hall on the way to class. He never stays angry very long and besides he knows he shouldn't be mad at me anyway. After all we fought those punks together and they're probably after me as much as they are after him, especially the one I clobbered with my mom's sanitary napkins. Much to my relief, I have not seen any sign of them since the battle. They may think we reported them to our parents and are staying scarce.

The school day drags on and when the final bell rings, I can't wait to get out and catch the bus to Elmwood where I'm meeting up with Bob, who's catching the bus up from his school in Cranston. He called me from his new guardian's house, and said he wanted to see me to tell me the latest news about his brother. When I pressed him to tell me on the phone, he said he wanted to tell me in person. It didn't sound like anything urgent, and I got the impression that mostly he just wanted to hang out, which was fine with me. It's been a long time since we've seen each other, and I'm curious about how his new life is going. He was feeling gloomy the last time we went ledge walking, when Emil almost fell down the transom.

There's quite a bit of snow on the ground and the wind is whipping around the school building so hard that I have to lean into it to move. Midway across the playground I slip on ice and go crashing into the piled snow. As I'm regaining my footing my eyes catch sight of what at first appears to be a mound of snow on top of the building's third floor window, but that's not what has caught my attention. Rather it was movement coming from it, and it's not like the wind was causing it to shift but like it was stirring from inside . . . breathing. I drift closer to the building for a better look, and that's when I see the white heap move again. It isn't snow at all, but something alive nestled against the bricks between the school's highest floor and roof.

For at least ten more minutes I try to understand what it is that's perched against the school's peak, and during that time there's no further movement from it. Whatever it is it's as if it has detected my presence and has decided to become totally still in case I am going to swoop up and grab it. The only thing I can figure that could reach that height is a bird, and the more I look at the object the more that makes sense, but what kind of a bird is at least a foot tall and almost pure white, I wonder? Whatever kind it is, it isn't like any I have ever seen.

By now I've been standing in the school lot for the better part of a half an hour and remember that Bob is waiting for me at our designated meeting place. I lock my eyes on the foreign object as I back away toward the street where I notice the city bus approaching that will take me to Elmwood. I swear to God the moment the bus pulls up the furry thing moves like it is relieved that I'm leaving.

Bob is standing in front of the dime store where we agreed to meet when I arrive, and although I'm obviously late, he doesn't complain but instead greets me with an expression verging on indifference.

By way of hello, I say "Dwadillypod," and he looks at me like I'm from Mars. "Hey, that's what you used to say all the time," I remind him kind of insulted by his reaction.

"Yeah, but it was stupid and really didn't mean anything, so I don't say it anymore. In fact, I kind of hate it now," replies Bob., and I feel rebuffed.

"Where did it come from?" I ask, and Bob says it was a word he made up when he was little and first realized his mother was insane.

"I guess you left all that back there," I say, pointing in the direction of Providence.

"Guess, so," answers Bob, his expression darkening.

With that we enter the dime store to get a soda at the lunch counter. Bob orders a cherry coke and I ask for one with vanilla syrup.

"Hey, you know what," asks Bob brightening a little, and I sense he has something really big to tell me.

"Mark's in jail," he says in a matter of fact tone.

"Why, because he beat you up?" I ask blowing into my straw to make the liquid in my glass froth up.

"No. He beat up Father Carter."

"Yeah, sure," I remark, thinking he's putting me on.

"No, I mean it. He went over to the church rectory, slipped inside, and pounded out the old perve. Broke his nose and two teeth. The housekeeper heard screams and called the cops. They caught Mark a block away and put him in the slammer. Now he's got to go to trial."

I can't believe what Bob's reporting, but I realize he's telling the truth.

"Why'd he do it?" I ask, wanting more details.

"When I saw him in jail he told me Father Carter had done sex things to him when he was in catechism for his First Holy Communion. He said he never told anyone because he was embarrassed and then our dad got killed and our mom got more nuts."

"What kind of things?" I ask, and Bob reports that his brother wouldn't get into it. "Must have been pretty disgusting to make him beat up Father Carter," I venture, and Bob agrees.

"Figure that's why he was always drinking and pissed off. He constantly had a chip on his shoulder about something. Ever since he was a kid."

Bob says he actually feels sorry for Mark now that he knows the truth and he plans to visit him in jail as long as he's there. I ask if I can go because I've never been in a real prison, and Bob says that only relatives are allowed to visit inmates. After talking a little bit more, Bob suddenly reports that he has to get back to Cranston to run an errand for his foster parents, and we shake hands and promise to meet again soon, but I secretly doubt I'll be seeing much of him, because he says he hates coming back to his old neighborhood.

By the time I get home it's dark and it feels colder than any time I can remember, but my father is standing out on the steps peering across the street. He's lost in thought and hardly notices me until I'm practically on top of him and then he snaps out of it.

"Davy, where've you been, kiddo? Kind of late to be getting in, don't you think?" and I tell him I met with Bob, even though I know it won't make him happy.

"That kid, jeez, what did I tell you?" he grumbles, and I tell him about what happened with Mark.

His reaction is not unexpected. "That guy is a bum and probably made the story up about that priest doing things to him. Bet he broke into the rectory to rob it and got caught by the Father. Look, he beat up his own kid brother, so who you going to believe, that sleeze or a priest?"

I'm about to tell him about all the sex things Father Carter says at confession but decide not to get into it because it would open up a whole other can of worms, I figure. Besides, I feel really tired and just want to grab something to eat and get under the covers to get the deep aching chill out of my bones.

A Real Nightmare

Sara has me cornered in the Polio House, and her tiny cold hand is pressed against my neck. She stares up at me with zombie yellow eyes, but her expression is more sad than scary, and for some weird reason I'm not frightened. The more I look at her the more I feel her sorrow and pain. Tears form in her vacant sockets and rush down her colorless cheeks. Without moving her lips she's saying something to me, something I can't make out, but the tone communicates distress and urgency. I want to help her, but I am at a loss for what to do. She's dead so what can I do, I think, and it doesn't disturb me that I'm standing in front of someone who's not alive.

Beyond the door to the room we occupy comes a loud rumble, like an earthquake, and I can detect the sour odor of smoke. In seconds the space we're in is sucked of its oxygen and the temperature becomes unbearably hot. Then the door crashes open and flames reach in for us. Sara lets out a cry and instead of trying to get away from the approaching fire, she turns and runs directly into it. Everything in me wants to follow, but I can't even move. My feet are riveted to the floor, as the fire stretches in my direction. My flesh begins to melt and drip to the floor like in the "House of Wax" and then I wake up, choking as I gasp for air.

I'm in my room, but something is flickering brightly outside my window, and I can smell smoke . . . real smoke.

"Davy, come on down!" I hear my father shout from the stairs that lead to the attic.

The realization that something terrible is actually happening takes hold of me. For a moment, like in my nightmare, I can't move, which makes me wonder if it's really over.

"What's the matter?" I finally manage to yell back to my father, who says we have to get out of the house because there's a fire.

I can't believe that our house is burning, especially coming out of the dream I just had, and when I descend to where my father is standing and throwing on his coat, he reports that the Polio House is on fire and that the firemen have instructed us to evacuate in case burning embers land on our house and light it up, too. He doesn't think that will happen because it's covered with snow. Just the same he says we better do as we're told.

Linda emerges from her room with her hair in rollers and a scowl on her face obviously none too pleased that her beauty rest has been disturbed. My mom is already downstairs fetching our coats and boots and my father bustles us along barking commands all the way.

"Move it faster, guys. Act like you're alive, for god sakes."

A fireman takes us to the fire station a few streets over where we can wait until the all clear is given and we can return home. My dad is not having any of that, and when we're dropped off at the station, he informs us that he's returning to our house to make sure no vandals break in. My mom protests, fearing he might get hurt, but he trudges off anyway.

"Damned if I'll wait around here so someone can rob us during all the commotion. It's the perfect opportunity for crooks."

I want to accompany him, but he tells me to take care of my sister and mother while he's gone. It's the first time I have been given that responsibility, and I feel a sense of pride that I'm in charge of their safety while he's gone. A couple hours later he returns, saying that we can go home and that the fire is out although there is nothing left of the Polio House. I ask him how he thinks the fire started, and he offers a couple possibilities.

"Who knows? Could be bad wiring. Maybe a drunk got in there. Thought I saw some activity in there at night a couple of times. Place was an accident waiting to happen. No big loss, though. Neighborhood's better off without that eyesore. I sure won't miss it."

Neither will I, I think to myself, glad I won't have to look out at it from my room any more, and I wonder if now that it's gone, little Sara will be gone, too? Recalling my nightmare it now strikes me as significant that she ran into the flames rather than away from them when the building was actually on fire in real life. Why it seems so meaningful, I can't quite fathom. It just does. Maybe the house burning down freed Sara to go to heaven. Could be that running through the flames put her right at the Pearly Gates. Could be she had to get through hell or maybe purgatory first. Until I fall asleep back home, a zillion theories enter my head about why Sara chose to dash into the fire but nothing makes total sense. The only thing I know for sure is that it's really hard to understand why ghosts do the things they do.

Suspicion Ignited

The Polio House is nothing but a heap of charred rubble and now visible in the space where it once stood is the backyard of the house on the next street over. I wake up with a nagging thought and on the way to school it's all I can think about. What if Henry set the Polio House on fire? He always has a box of matches with him and he loves to play with them, I reason. He nearly set the asylum on fire tons of times, I recall, and he's mad about being punched in the face by that white kid. Plus, like his uncles told him, there are those poor black people whose houses were set on fire by bigots. The possibility that he did it grows in my mind to the point that I'm almost certain he's guilty by the time I reach school.

I need to know if Henry did it. I find him in the cafeteria with his Chinese friend and ask him if he'll meet me after school. At first he barely acknowledges me but then nods okay to my request. We're to meet in the field next to the school, and I go directly there as soon as the final bell rings. Knowing the way Henry moves, I figure I'll be waiting a while before he shows, and then I wonder if he'll show up at all. While I'm waiting I remember the creature that was perched on top of the school building and look in its direction. Sure enough it's still there and not moving a lick like before. My curiosity about it almost makes me forget Henry, who pops out of nowhere and shouts my name so I about jump into his arms. Swear to God I think I'm going to have a heart attack.

"Boy, you sure do scare easily," he laughs, and for a moment things seem like they used to be when we were hanging out together.

"Check it out," I say, pointing to whatever it is up on the building.

"Looks like some kind of miniature snowman. How'd it get up there?" he asks scooping up a chunk of ice and rearing back to heave it at the thing.

"Don't," I say blocking his throw. "Leave it alone. It's not bothering anything."

"Scuse me, Mr. Future Veterin . . . er, animal doctor," he replies sarcastically, reluctantly dropping the ice. "So why you want to talk?" he asks with a frown.

I take a deep breath and put the question to him.

His eyes widen and he takes a step backward as if someone has shoved him. "You're nuts!" he exclaims.

"Well, I just thought . . . " I mumble before he cuts me off, his expression transformed into one of anger and defiance.

"What if I did? You going to turn me in to the police? Just like a white boy thinking all coloreds are criminals. You're some friend, Ketch! Shhiiit!" he spits.

He then removes his familiar box of matches from his coat pocket, lights one, and flicks it at me. Before I can react he turns and trudges away leaving me more confused than ever.

On my way home I drop by Mary Kay's as I promised and she's all smiles because she's learned her dad will be coming home sooner than expected. About to bubble over with excitement she reports he'll be home in one or two days and I say that's great.

"I've really missed him and mom has, too," she says, and I ask where her mom is. "Out to the store," she replies. She'll be back soon."

We move to the living room but on the way Mary Kay places her crutches against a table and takes the last couple of steps on her own. I congratulate her on her progress, and she reports that she has taken as many as six steps without her crutches. She plans to greet her dad without the crutches when he comes through the door.

"What happened at the Polio House?" she asks when we reach the couch, and I fill her in on how we had to go to the fire station and stay until the fire was put out. "My mom says it doesn't surprise her given all the tragedy there. Do you think it was that little girl ghost who did it?"

"No," I answer and then tell her my suspicions. "It might have been Henry. I mean, I don't know for sure, but he's always playing with matches and almost burned down the asylum. Besides, he's been really mad at things lately because he got beat up by those guys in the hot rod I told you about."

"Gee, what're you going to do?" asks Mary Kay her eyes widening from my revelation.

"I can't prove it, and maybe he didn't do it, but I keep thinking he did," I answer, and she says that if I think so I should report it to the police because I'll be what she calls an accessory after the fact if I don't.

"I heard someone hiding a criminal called that on TV," she reports.

"Yeah," I agree. "I've already thought of that, too, but if I'm wrong then it's going to be a whole mess, and if I'm right Henry is going to go to jail. So I don't know."

"Did you tell your parents? Maybe they'll know what to do," she offers, her voice full of concern.

The more we talk the more flustered I become about the whole situation and then I feel like I just need to be alone to figure things out. I say goodbye and walk the half block home, my eyes glued to the burned remains of the Polio House.

Going for Good

By the time I meet up with Corey down at Haven's Diner a couple days later, my suspicion that Henry may have burned down the Polio House is just as strong and maybe stronger, although nothing solid has come up to make me feel that way. It's just that the more I think about how Henry has been acting lately, the more my instincts point to him as the arsonist.

Before I can get into it with Corey, he has news of his own. He's leaving for Australia much sooner than he thought, and he may not even finish out the school year in Providence. When I ask him about missing school he says he won't lose any class time.

"The school year is not exactly the same down there as it is up here, so I won't really miss anything. You know that it's late summer there right now? The seasons are reversed down there. Lots of things aren't like they are here. The water even turns a different way when it goes down the drain," he says, clearly relishing the prospect of moving to such an exotic place, and I wish my family could move there, too.

For a while he goes on about all the strange animals in Australia and how a game called Cricket is a popular sport there until I cut in and tell him about the Polio House burning to the ground.

"No crap?" he says dumbfounded and wanting to go check it out right away. "How'd that happen?"

"Well . . ." I say, taking a deep breath before I unload with my theory that Henry set it on fire, "I have a bad feeling that Henry did it."

Corey gives me a long hard look and then asks why I think that.

"Because he's a pyromaniac," I answer using a word I've discovered in a book in the school library when looking up information about arsonists.

"A pyromaniac?" asks Corey, and I explain to him what it is, although he says he kind of knew what it meant. "How do you know he's that?" continues Corey skeptically.

"You remember how he almost set the asylum on fire, and acted crazy with matches, right?" I say by way of an answer, adding, "He said he'd like to burn some white people's houses down because they set fire to poor black people's places in the south. Then he's been really angry about the white kid punching him in the face, and he says his mom doesn't want him hanging out with people who aren't colored anymore."

Corey digests my comments for a moment and then agrees that it's possible, although he still doubts it.

"Henry's a little crazy, but I don't think he'd do anything that nuts," he says, gulping down the last of his three hot dogs.

He considers going to look at what's left of the Polio House and then decides against it, saying he promised his mom he'd get home early to help her clear out the basement in preparation of their move. For a time my thoughts about the fire and Henry are replaced by my concern over losing Corey to the other side of the world.

"Will you ever come back?" I ask as we leave the diner, and Corey says probably not until we're both grown up.

The prospect of this really gives me the blues, and when I get home my dad notices my gloom. I tell him about Corey moving away, and he comments that life is full of disappointments and I should get used to it.

"It's a pisser out there, kid, so brace yourself for more kicks in the head. You'll get over them though. Believe me."

He's sipping a bottle of Narragansett beer, which is no surprise because he's been drinking more and more lately, even though my mom doesn't like it and he made a promise not to. He catches my disapproval and looks embarrassed.

"Don't worry. This stuff doesn't taste as good to me as it used to," he says, and puts the bottle down next to his chair. "Maybe I'll go back to soda pop. There's some in the icebox if you want it. I brought home a quart of Orange Nehi."

"I think I know how the fire got started, I say, surprised to hear myself admit that to him.

"What?" replies my father with an odd expression like he's as surprised to hear me say that as I am for saying it.

"I been thinking and I believe the Polio . . . ah, I mean the house across the street was set on fire."

"No one set that trap on fire," responds my father with sudden agitation. "Place was a bonfire waiting to happen. Probably leaky gas pipes or crappy wiring set it off. Happens all the time. Stop imagining things, Davy."

"Well, I don't think so," I say and my father's forehead gets all crinkly as it does when he gets upset.

"So Sherlock, who torched the joint?"

"I think Henry did," I reply feeling a jab of remorse about having to tell on a friend.

"Henry?" my father asks perplexed.

Over the next few minutes I run down the list of reasons why I suspect Henry set the Polio House on fire while my father listens attentively.

"Sounds like you've been doing a lot of thinking about this. I thought Henry was your buddy," my father comments after I finish my testimony.

"He is, but I don't think he should have done it," I reply defensively feeling like I have just been caught ratting on somebody.

"That's if he did do it, Davy. You don't know that for sure."

I'm a little surprised and disappointed that my father is not immediately won over by my argument, since he has no affection for Henry.

"Well, maybe I should go talk to the police about it anyway," I suggest, and my father says that would be dumb since I have no evidence.

"You're just going to get yourself in trouble by making accusations you can't prove," he continues reminding me of Mr. Brennan's views about the Clayburgh letter.

"I'm going anyway, I say," and my father erupts telling me I'm not going to do any such thing and to go to my room. "Fine," I shout on my way upstairs to the attic, adding that I just wanted to do what I thought was right.

"Right is not getting people in trouble based on nothing but a suspicion," my father yells after me.

My room is freezing, so as usual I don't even bother removing my clothes before I get in bed. Soon I doze off and in my trouble dreams I see the giant white bird that's perched on my school building, and it looks so miserable and alone I want to rescue it and take it back to where it came from. The need to help it takes deep root in me. I also dream of going to Corey's house and ringing the doorbell, but no one answers, and I realize that he's gone forever.

Coming Clean

In the middle of the night the sound of my bedroom door creaking open awakes me with a chill, and I hold my breath waiting for something horrible to enter hoping it's not little Sara back from beyond the flames.

"Davy, are you awake?" whispers my father, and I exhale.

"What's the matter, dad?" I ask, fearing there's another fire.

"Just wanted to talk to you for a minute, okay?"

He comes over and sits on the edge of my bed. "Cold in here, buddy," he says, and I think no kidding while remaining wrapped in my blanket.

"Got to fix that radiator or find out why it doesn't get any heat," he says and then takes a long pause before starting to talk again. "Look, I don't want you telling people you think Henry started the fire. I know you have your reasons for thinking he did, but you're wrong about it, and it will only cause trouble."

Then there is kind of a long silence. Then I say, "Okay," so he'll leave. I'm about to fall asleep when my dad says, "I burned that house down."

The weight on my lids is lifted instantly as I try to process what I think I just heard.

"WHAT?" I ask thinking what I heard was a part of a dream slipping up on me.

"I had my reasons, but that doesn't make it right," he says. "I thought it would make things better if that ugly place was gone. Better for the neighborhood and better for you kids who thought it was haunted."

When his words finally sink in, I'm stunned.

"You swear to God, dad? You really did?"

"I know this is a shock but you have to promise to say nothing to anybody, not even your sister or mother. Will you do that? If you don't it's going to cause us all real trouble."

"But it's a crime," I respond my words muffled by the bed sheet over my mouth.

"Not really," he replies in a slightly irritated tone. "Not if it was done to make things better for us and the neighborhood."

"What if someone was in there, maybe a bum? They could have died," I remark trying to come to terms with what he is saying.

"No one was in there, believe me. I checked the whole place from top to bottom and then some."

"Still," I reply, about to challenge this when he cuts me off.

"Okay, I know it wasn't a good thing to do, but it just got to me seeing everything falling apart for us because that dump was ruining the neighborhood and killing property values. People are moving in all around here because it's so cheap, and they're the kind of people that keep it cheap and make it more run down. Maybe it wasn't the right way to go about it, but I didn't know any other way. Just didn't want things to get worse around here."

"But now its all burnt down and looks even worse," I protest, and he says at least no undesirables will be moving in right across the street from us.

"Look," he says rising from my bed, "I'm sorry, okay, but just keep this between you and me and everything will be alright. Go back to sleep," he says making his way out of my room and closing the creaky door behind him.

Whatever sleepiness I felt has completely left me as I attempt to digest the fact that my own father is the arsonist and not Henry. Things have just gotten worse, I sense, peering in the direction of my window which now looks out on my father's crime scene.

About Dads

Several days have gone by and my dad's shocking confession is about the only thing on my mind. The only other thing is the big white creature at school. I've discovered in a book on birds that it's a Snowy Owl from way up in the Arctic. It has not moved from the top of the building yet and it's been several days, maybe longer. I'm concerned that it must be starving because I don't think it leaves the window ledge to hunt for food. At least not when I have seen it, and it would be hunting during the day, according to the book. I read that it feeds on something called lemmings, and I'm not sure there are any around South Providence. It's a male, too, because the book says they're almost pure white, and he is as white as the snow surrounding him.

When I point out the owl to other kids, they only seem slightly interested, and that surprises me since it's not an animal that people often see as far down as Rhode Island. The book says they do occasionally migrate as far south as Quebec in search of food when winters are really bad way up north, but Canada is a long way off, too. I'm fascinated by other facts I read about the Snowy Owl, such as when they make a sound, which they seldom do, it comes out like a dog bark and they can swivel their heads almost totally around. The one up on the school building has yet to do either to my disappointment.

I've told Mary Kay about the stranded owl, and she says she's going to get her dad to take her to school to see it. He retuned from the sea yesterday, and on my way home I catch sight of Mary Kay and her father walking in front of their house. They move slowly up the street, and her dad is carrying her crutches. I figure this is her big moment to impress him about how well she has recovered, and I deliberately slow down so I don't distract her. She's doing great but suddenly begins to tip to her side and her father grabs and steadies her. They both clutch each other and then her dad lets go and she continues walking on her own. A few more steps, and her dad cheers her accomplishment by whooping loudly and twirling his hat. Even though Mary Kay can't see me, I can see her beaming expression. I decide to let them have their privacy and take a short cut to my house through some backyards. My dad is wrestling with the frozen trashcans when I arrive.

"Damn things are stuck to the ground," he grunts, and asks me how I'm doing.

This is the first real contact I've had with him since the night in my room, and I feel like I really haven't got anything to say to him. I'm still all confused about what he did. Out of the blue, he says he's contemplating turning himself in to the cops, and without thinking I register my opposition to the idea.

"Why? You said that it would mess everything up, and what about mom? She's still getting over polio. It will make her sick again."

"It wasn't right what I did, and it sure doesn't set a good example for you. I didn't want you to get Henry in trouble, so I told you. Now it's something you got to live with, too, and it's just not fair. Maybe they'll go light on me for fessing up."

"They'll still send you to jail, and we'll all be left alone without you," I continue to protest.

"It just seems that it's something I should do to make things right. I don't want you thinking your old man is a louse. People do dumb things sometimes thinking it's the right thing. What I did was dumb and wasn't right."

"You're not a louse," I reply touching his arm with my mitten. "Besides no one was hurt and nothing valuable was lost. You said the neighborhood is better off now, so that's not a crime. Maybe you shouldn't have set it on fire, but nothing really bad happened, right?"

"But it could have," replies my father shaking his head. "It could have."

For a moment we stand in the backyard without exchanging any other words, then my dad grabs a hold of me and squeezes me tightly.

"You're a heck of a good kid, Davy," he says, and I feel a big lump in my throat.

Ladies Day

On Friday we get our report cards, and Linda has gotten straight A's. My mom is celebrating by making Linda's favorite dinner—stuffed pork chops and vanilla wafer pudding for dessert. I like both of them, too, so I benefit from her classroom performance. I did okay as well, with mostly B's, even with my cuts, but Linda is definitely the scholar in the family, says mom holding up her grade card like it's a trophy, and I guess to her it is. She wants us both to go to college, but we'll need to do exceptional in order to get money awarded to us so we can, since our parents can't afford it.

"If you do this in your junior and senior years, you'll get to go to a really good college," says mom cheerily moving around the kitchen preparing Linda's reward. "You get those grades up there a little more, David, and you'll go to a fine school, too."

"I'll try," I promise, and my mom says if I do she's sure I'll succeed.

"We've got two really smart kids here, Mr. Ketchum."

"That's a fact," responds my father, who is peeling potatoes for the feast in Linda's honor. "They're going to set the world on fire," he says and then I can tell by his expression that he realizes the irony of his words, which are not lost on me either. "Yeah, you kids will do just great," he adds with much less bounce in his voice.

It still bothers me a whole lot what he did, because it was a crime and not a little one either. Even though I love my father, I feel like he really shouldn't get away with what he did, but then his going to jail would hurt all of us, and that doesn't seem fair either. I know he's really disturbed about setting the Polio House on fire, and I figure that's a kind of punishment in itself. Besides this is as happy as I've seen my mother since before she got sick, and her face has regained the prettiness that the polio had all but taken away. In fact it dawns on me that Linda looks a lot like her. They both have thick wavy brown hair and big green eyes that twinkle when they smile. Right now they both look really beautiful, which is something I'd tell my mom but not my sister.

We're told to get out of the kitchen while the celebration dinner is being prepared, and we adjourn to the front room to watch "The Mouseketeers" on our crummy TV set. Given the good mood of our parents I think this may be a smart time to make another pitch for a new television, but my sister advises against it because she plans to ask our mom to loan her a bunch of her S&H Green Stamps to finally get the transistor radio she's been so desperate for.

"If I can get two more pages of stamps, I'll have enough for the RCA portable," she confides.

"Can I use it sometimes?" I ask, expecting her to say no as usual, but this time she surprises me.

"Maybe, if I'm not using it."

Of course, when she's not using it could mean never, I realize, but I decide not to push it to avoid changing her mood, too. It really seems good to have everyone cheerful for a change. As we sit together trying to make out which Mouseketeer it is on the bleary screen, I'm tempted to spill the beans about dad setting the Polio House on fire, but I know if there's anything that will turn the mood sour, it would be that. Being the only one in the family who knows the truth about it is hard, but I promised my father to keep quiet and I will. Instead of sharing that unpleasant secret with her, I tell her about the Snowy Owl at school. At first she doesn't seem all that interested, but when I explain how rare it is and that it's from the Arctic she begins to pay more attention.

"What's it doing down here?" she asks, and I say probably looking for food. "Then why is it just staying on top of the building and not searching for something to eat?"

"I don't know," I confess, adding that it may be hurt or possibly can't find any food it likes and is now too exhausted to look anymore.

"Maybe you should tell your teacher or principal so someone can help it," she offers becoming more serious.

"Maybe I will," I reply, but really have no intention of doing so because I'm pretty sure they'll trap it and take it to the zoo, which would mean it would never get home to the Arctic again.

We sit quietly for a few more minutes as the grainy figures on the TV sing their farewell song, and then Linda brings up what I said about her showing off her boobs to boys.

"Whoever told you that is a big fat liar. I never did that, and I never will. Not until I get married, I mean. That Henry friend of yours tells things that are really awful," she says with a frown forming on her face.

"I didn't believe it anyway," I say, which isn't a lie because I really didn't think she would do that. "Henry just says things to get a rise out of people. Nobody believed him. I swear to god."

"Well, he shouldn't have said it in the first place. Things like that get around and hurt people even if they're not true."

I apologize to Linda for Henry's dirty story about her, thinking now I'll have to apologize to Henry for accusing him of setting fire to the Polio House.

From on High

The first thought in my head when I wake up the next morning is about saving the Snowy Owl if he's still up on the school building. It's a Teacher's Day so school is out, and I view this as an opportunity to attempt a rescue. Before going to sleep the night before I concoct a plan to save the Arctic bird. It involves climbing to the roof and lowering food to it with a piece of twine. The only problem with my plan is that I don't have the kind of food Snowy Owls usually eat. I have no idea how to get a hold of lemmings so I gather a bunch of stuff from our icebox, including a left over pork chop, some old sardines in mustard sauce, and two slices of baloney that I hope will substitute.

The schoolyard is empty when I arrive and sure enough the giant owl hasn't moved an inch and I wonder if it has frozen solid. My route up to the roof involves jumping as high as I can into the air and hooking the fire escape ladder with an umbrella the way I did at the Dorrance Street building where Emil almost croaked. My strategy when I get to the top is to go to a place just over where the bird is perched and then lower some food to it. I'm not sure it will eat what I have but figure it's better than letting it just starve up there.

My Gargoyle experience comes in handy and without any hitches I'm up on the roof looking out over the houses that surround the school. I crouch down as I move to the side of the building to where the owl is located to keep out of sight in case someone spots me before I can fulfill my mission. When I peak over the side of the roof the owl rotates its head in my direction and we make eye contact. His yellow eyes remind me of little Sara's in my nightmare when she ran into the flames. For a moment I consider the possibility that her spirit has taken up residence in the bird recalling a story about Eskimos who believed a little girl was changed into an owl. These thoughts are broken when the owl lets out a squeaky bark that makes me jump and I set to work wrapping the pork chop to lower it to the hungry critter.

From my lofty location I can see teachers entering the main entrance of the building, so I hold off what I'm doing until the coast is clear. I then lower the meat to the owl, whose head moves back and forth as it dangles in front of it. A few minutes pass before I decide to haul in the chop and try the baloney. The bird's reaction is the same, no takers. It just stares with its big yellow eyes at the flap of pink meat that dangles in front of its beak without making any attempt to sample it. It doesn't go for the sardines either, and I'm at a loss about what to do next.

Teachers continue to arrive for their meeting as I hide out on the roof trying to come up with another plan to save the owl. It doesn't make sense to bring him any more food from home, I conclude. It's lemmings or nothing for this wild animal. My fear that it may starve to death fills me with greater urgency and I decide to try to capture it. I have no idea what I'll do once I get it, but leaving it to die a lonely and horrible death on top of the old school building seems a cruel thing to do.

After a few minutes I decide to shimmy down to the ledge and wrap the bird in my overcoat and hoist it and myself back on the roof. That won't be easy, I realize, but it seems like the only possible way to get it out of its dire situation. As I swing my leg over the ledge, I spot more teachers, so I freeze in place until they disappear inside the building. When I drag my other leg over the ledge my whole body drops toward the owl, narrowly missing its head, and I almost loose my grip on the roof. *So this is what it feels like to fall off a building, I think.* The owl lets out another weird bark and then spreads its wings and glides off the window top. I hang there watching as it rapidly plunges toward the ground, and I'm certain it's going to crash against the icy pavement, but at the last minute it swoops upward avoiding certain death.

With all my might I manage to pull myself back onto the roof all the while watching the owl's skyward flight. It climbs and climbs toward the puffy white clouds and gradually disappears over the northern horizon, and I'm elated and relieved. I feel like a huge weight has been lifted from me, because in my mind the owl's fate had somehow become tied to my own. It may sound funny but I had come to believe if the creature could get back home then everything would be okay in my world, too. On my way down the fire escape, I see the principal, Mr. Walling, approaching the building and figure I'm in trouble because he's looking straight in my direction, but it's as if I'm invisible because he just continues into the building.

Things Change

Over a year has passed since the Snowy Owl flew away from certain doom on the school building and back to its Arctic home. Lots have changed since then and mostly for the better, I think. Best of all is that a doctor named Salk has invented a shot to keep people from getting polio, so kids won't be crippled and have to use crutches and wheelchairs. I think it's sad that it was discovered too late for Mary Kay, but I'm glad others like her and adults like my mom won't get the disease.

A new house now stands where the Polio House once was. A family from Puerto Rico moved in, which didn't make my dad too happy until he found out that the father worked as an electrician at the university where he works. They had already met there and when my dad realized he was our new neighbor his attitude about the family changed. In fact, my dad and Mr. Estevez have become good friends, and they spend a lot of time in Mr. Estevez's garage where he has a workshop. Even Mr. Brennan drops in there occasionally when he feels okay. I hear a lot of laughing coming from the garage and it makes me really happy. They're drawing up plans to build a fallout shelter in back of the Estevez's house so we can all be saved if the Commies attack. Dad is still bothered by what he did, and I think it's scared him into going back to church. My mother has heard that Father Carter has been reassigned to a church in Massachusetts, and we all like his replacement at St. John's, including my dad. I'm just glad he doesn't ask any creepy questions in confession, and I'd like him even better if he didn't give out such long Acts of Contrition. I wonder how many Hail Mary's and Our Father's my dad had to say for burning down the Polio House? Probably hundreds, I calculate. He doesn't drink beer anymore and doesn't get angry when I hang out with Henry, who spends quite a bit of time in my attic room these days. Dad doesn't say anything to get Henry upset like he used to, but I know he'd just as soon I hang out with someone else. Still, Henry is a good friend and to make things even better he likes the kid our age that moved in across the street, although he teases him about his name.

"Roberto," he laughs, "That's a pretty one. Sounds kinda' girlie to me."

When Roberto tells him that his nickname is Bo, Henry calls him Bobo, and sometimes booby, but that doesn't seem to bother our new companion, who appears more amused by Henry's goofy behavior than disturbed by it. Henry is always going to be Henry, I guess. His mom lets me come over, even though she's not exactly thrilled about him hanging out with a white kid, he tells me, but she acts pretty friendly, so I'm wondering if Henry has exaggerated that whole thing. What I like most about being at Henry's is when I'm invited to stay for dinner. I still can't get enough of his mom's incredible cooking.

Mary Kay is walking much better but she still needs crutches, and my mom says she probably always will. We're closer than ever now that she's back at school, and when I'm not hanging out with Henry and Bo, I'm with her. Henry says even with her twisted legs, she gives him a cukey because she is one of the prettiest white girls he's ever seen, and I agree. I hardly notice her leg braces anymore. To me she's like every other normal kid, except she's a very special one to me. I think we have become boyfriend and girlfriend more than just ordinary friends. We're both only fifteen, but I think we were made for each other.

The other day I got a postcard from Corey in Australia. He says he loves it there but misses Providence sometimes, especially the Haven Brother's chilidogs. His mom has got engaged to someone he likes who owns an airplane and flies them into someplace called the Outback where he's seen lots of wild animals, including kookaburras and wallabies, whatever they are. What cheers me up most about his postcard is his statement about returning for a visit later in the summer. He'll be coming back with his mom who has to meet with realtors about selling the house she still owns in South Providence. Even though I've grown a couple inches in the last year, I figure Corey is now over six feet tall. I still don't have a beard, but I can imagine how thick his has become. He tells me to say hello to Bob and Emil, who I've only seen a couple of times the last year.

Bob's got a different life in Cranston and he doesn't seem all that keen on getting together anymore. When we do he isn't his old self. I think it's the bad memories he has back here. He says his brother is due to get out of jail in another six months and is going to Florida to get a job on a fishing boat. He doesn't want anything else to do with Providence either, I figure.

On a rainy day in late April I spot Bob standing at a bus stop. He is holding a brown paper bag and it occurs to me that it contains a bottle of wine and that he came up from Cranston to get a bum to buy it for him at the local liquor store where we did the same thing with Corey. Instead of saying hello, I turn and walk in the opposite direction figuring he is not interested in seeing me.

When I run into Emil, he asks if I've been doing any more ledge walking and I tell him those days are behind me. I guess I knew that when I almost fell on top of the Snowy Owl. Emil says it's something he'll never do again either, and we both agree that ledge walking on top of tall buildings is a pretty stupid activity. We're trying to come up with something that's not as dangerous but proves we have more courage than the average kid. We might go back to tumbling down hills in cardboard boxes because at least you risk breaking some bones that way. Emil suggests we take turns shooting his scooter off one of the hills, but I'm not sure about that.

My nightmares pretty much stopped around the time the Snowy Owl flew away and I'm sure there's a connection. The other night I had a dream that started like a nightmare though. In it I was awakened by something beckoning me from outside my window. It reminded me of all of the times when the Polio House was still across the street and I felt an awful darkness waiting to suck me in. Yet this time it was different. I wasn't scared like before. Instead, I was anxious to get to the window to see what it was that was drawing me to it. There, in the second floor window of the new house, stood little Sara, and she was smiling.

MISSING FAMILY FOUND

***Providence*–** Authorities say they have located the whereabouts of the Clayburgh family of South Providence. Reported missing in July 1953, Calvin and Martina Clayburgh and their two children have been found in Henderson, Tennessee, where they joined relatives in the operation of a small foundry. The family's youngest child, Sara, succumbed to polio months before they left the area. The Clayburghs are reportedly doing well and have no plans to return to the city. The house they occupied at 147 Belmont Street was destroyed by fire last year.

(Providence Tribune,
May 12, 1955)

AUTHOR BIOGRAPHY-

Michael C. Keith, Ph.D., is the author of over 20 books on the electronic media, including Radio Cultures, Sounds in the Dark, Talking Radio, and the acclaimed text The Radio Station, now in its eighth edition. He is the cofounder of the Radio Division of the Broadcast Education Association and its first chair. His memoir (The Next Better Place) won critical praise from reviewers around the country. Keith is also the author of many short stories, which have appeared in various webzines and journals. He teaches Communication at Boston College and is the recipient of several accolades for his scholarship in radio studies, among them the IRTS's Stanton Fellow Award and BEA's Distinguished Scholar Award.